The Great Chase

he clamored as he ran out the porch. "He's after me . . . and my horse!"

"You don't need a rifle," answered Chatfield quietly. "You're our guest, Mister Lightfoot . . . I'll attend to Val Bodie myself."

He strode out to the gate and without a word of warning raised his gun to his shoulder and fired. The bullet struck up the dust in front of a galloping horseman, and Lightfoot recognized Bodie. He was mounted on Fly, and far down the road Johnny could see six other night riders. They had followed on his trail after their defeat at the gateway, wild with anger and the lust to kill.

Rider of
Death Valley

DANE
COOLIDGE

LEISURE BOOKS NEW YORK CITY

A LEISURE BOOK®

August 2009

Published by special arrangement with Golden West Literary Agency.

Dorchester Publishing Co., Inc.
200 Madison Avenue
New York, NY 10016

ISBN 10: 0-8439-6276-3
ISBN 13: 978-0-8439-6276-5
E-ISBN: 978-1-4285-0718-0

The name "Leisure Books" and the stylized "L" with design are
trademarks of Dorchester Publishing Co., Inc.

Printed in the United States of America.

10 9 8 7 6 5 4 3 2 1

Visit us online at www.dorchesterpub.com.

Rider of
Death Valley

Chapter One

Down a long, rocky wash, where round boulders as smooth as death's-heads lay shimmering in the heat, a train of covered wagons wound its way into the west, pounding a road out with grinding wheels. Behind, by the bitter waters of the Amargosa and up through a battle-strewn pass, lay the ruins of smoking wagons, unburied dead, and the litter of a losing fight. On their flanks a horde of Indians followed along, waiting for the end—and their loot.

The gaunt oxen, straining and groaning at the weight of their yokes, moved slowly, barely lifting their hoofs, although the bullwhips popped like pistol shots. They balked, rolling their eyes at the brazen sky and the pitiless desert peaks. Then, at a whiff of wind from the far abyss below, they lowed and surged on crazily. There was water in the sink that opened up before them—water that seethed and gave off steam like a caldron in the heat, water that gleamed like burnished silver in the sun. But to drink was to sup with death.

In the lead, as crazed with heat as the oxen they belabored, rushed young men in their prime and old men full of years, helter-skelter in their race for a drink. Twenty wagons, bumping and rumbling and grinding against the rocks, poured out from the cañon's mouth and crashed down the long slope that ended on the edge of the marsh. Behind

and moving slowly—with the train, but not a part
of it—there followed a wagon equipped with bar-
rels for water and guarded by one man with a rifle.
He was tall and eagle-eyed, with a long, black
beard, and he was mounted on a horse such as
never had been seen in the West. It was a stallion,
as yellow as gold, with a flowing mane and tail
and a small head on a high-crested neck, and, led
behind the wagon, were three more of that royal
strain that comes from the deserts of Arabia. Each
was yellow as gold; each had slim, springy legs
and the long, graceful lines of speed; each held its
head as if conscious still of the regal blood in its
veins. Begotten of the desert, they had returned at
last to a land even sterner than their own.

Between mountains so boldly sheer that they
rose like sun-blacked walls, there lay a valley below the level of the sea. In its sink the bitter waters
of a hundred desert draws lay steaming in a putrid
marsh. Broad quicksands, white and quivering,
merged at last with salt-caked flats, flanked by sand-
dhills where the wind leaped and played.

Then the mountains began, where from narrow-
mouthed cañons great boulders as big as houses
had been spouted out like pebbles before the resistless drive of cloudbursts. But on the floor of the
storm-swept washes brittle shrubs had reared their
heads and Selim, the stallion, champed at their tops
as he passed. Strange memories had come back to
him, latent instincts that could not die. He sniffed
the desert wind and sighed.

Across the flats at a lumbering gallop the twenty
wagons raced, leaving Randolph Morgan behind,
but, when they reached the marsh where the putrid waters gleamed, they mired in the treacherous

sands. There was no place for miles where man or beast could drink, and the hovering Indians yelled exultantly. Yet with desperate haste the leaders dug out their teams and followed hastily along the shore to the north.

The ground became firm; low hills rose before them where the mountains pressed in on the marshes. Between meadows of salt grass a winding creek could be seen, where the water drained in from the west. It was like a mirage, with green trees that danced and beckoned on the margin of a winding stream, and, as the oxen snuffled the breeze, they surged into their yokes and ran up the valley, bellowing.

Yet for all their frenzied haste, one wagon was ahead of them as they ascended the last, long slope. Randolph Morgan, the stranger who had followed in their rear, had cut across the flats while they were stuck. Leaving his wife to drive the oxen, he went galloping up the hill to look out over the valley below, and the Indians scattered before him like quail. Yet, although they scattered, they did not flee, and from the summit of a black butte they gazed down at him, watchful and expectant.

On the edge of the crystal stream that meandered through the meadow, Morgan knelt to slake his thirst. His lips were parched and cracking, his tongue swollen, his throat dry, but, as he bowed down to drink, Selim sniffed at the water and threw up his head with a snort. Morgan tasted—the water was salt. Yet, salty as it was, it was sweet to heat-parched lips and he threw himself down to drink. But once more, head by Morgan's head, Selim sniffed at the sparkling stream and his flaring nostrils snorted the alarm. With eyes that seemed to speak, he met his master's gaze, and Morgan spat the poisoned water back.

It was too clear, too clean, too devoid of vegetation and the scum of green, microscopic plants. There was a rank, fishy odor and a taste like Epsom salts, and the banks were dull, leprous white. Morgan rose up with a curse and gazed across at the swarming Indians, who were dancing on the butte top like crows. Even now they counted him dead.

Over the brow of the hill covered wagons came lumbering and dipped down into the valley below, while the drivers set up a cheer. But as the ox teams rushed forward, Randolph Morgan rode to meet them, waving his arms to turn them away.

"Don't drink!" he yelled. "The water is poison! Don't drink! It will be your death!" But the drivers did not give him a glance.

For two days and two nights they had been without water, more than the little in their casks and canteens. Their tongues were dry with thirst, their throats were choking, their bodies were too parched to sweat. Gaunt and emaciated, their eyes blinded by heat and dust, they drove madly down the hill and out across the flat toward the creek that flowed by, crystal-clear.

Men and oxen alike plunged into the little stream and drank deeply, although the water was salt. They wallowed in the mud in an ecstasy of relief, while their dried-up skins soaked in moisture. The man who rode among them, with warning shouts that the water was bad, was thought to be crazed by the heat. Teams of oxen, dragging their chains, came running from the wagons where their drivers had turned them loose and dammed the shallow stream with their bodies.

The covered wagons gave up women, with children at their skirts, and, as they knelt by the trampled shore, the strange man snatched them back, while he begged them not to drink. But they laughed and drank their fill, and at last he gave up in despair. Over the hill, struggling stubbornly against gad and brakes, his own oxen came in sight and he galloped to turn them back.

It was a battle from the start. The smell of water was in their nostrils, and they saw nothing of the death scene below. Already yokes of oxen, turned out to graze on the salt grass, had fallen like logs on the flats. The men who drove them were sickening now, stretched out in the shade of the wagons, yet still the one team that had been saved from their fate struggled and pawed and surged at their chains. Morgan fought them till he was weary, then threw the bull chain loose and let them go their way.

"Let them drink!" he called to his wife. "Let them die with the rest. We'll never escape alive if we wait on these cursed oxen. We must mount our horses, and ride!"

He threw a saddle on Neysa, his wife's gentle mare, and loaded the two fillies with food. And then, from the shaded wagon, he lifted out a baby and placed it in its mother's arms. On the flats below men were running in crazy circles or digging holes in the sand. They were sick, deathly sick, yet to quench their fevered thirst they crawled back to the creek to drink. The Indians, like flapping crows, swarmed the top of the grim, black butte, impatiently awaiting the end.

A fierce wind, furnace-hot, swept down from the north, seizing the sand of the giant dunes and hurling it on high like a pillar of smoke and flame. Then the sandstorm overwhelmed them, drawing a veil over their agonies as they ran in wider circles and fell. The Indians crept closer, eager to begin the work of looting, and with anger akin to madness Morgan charged down upon them, both pistols smoking at once. They fled to their black-domed butte, waving their arms exultantly. All was theirs—the desert had killed for them.

Chapter Two

Past sand dunes that came rolling on like the surf of a waterless sea, lashed about at the mercy of sudden, howling winds that whipped their crests to a spume, past trees stripped naked until their roots lay in gnarls, and others buried almost to their tips, past clay-formed, painted hills beneath a lurid, dust-smudged sky, they toiled on—father and mother and child. He rode on ahead, his black beard tossed by the gale, his keen eyes glowing with rage. Behind, like furtive shadows, the Indians dogged his steps, falling back when he turned to shoot at them.

Such horses as he rode had never been seen in the valley of Timbooshah. Behind them there was loot, wagonloads for the taking; but here were four horses that could run like the wind, and their hides were yellow as gold. Although his eyes gleamed vengefully, Randolph Morgan took no thought of the savages skulking behind. They were no more than the foxes who watched him from the hilltops. Another enemy was clutching at his throat.

Green trees rose up to mock him, there was rank grass on the flats, but water there was none, and the baby at breast cried fretfully and beat her hands. A great valley opened before them, walled in by shadowy mountains that caught the last rays of the sun. But where in all that vastness was there a spring to quench their thirst, a water hole not poisoned with salts? A dim trail led on along the base of the eastern hills, where wild burros had padded out a path. Where did these asses of the desert drink, and how could they find water at night?

Darkness came, and the man bowed his head to the saddle horn. The cries of the baby were stilled. Then the bridle rein fell slackly and Selim, son of the desert, sniffed the wind and turned to the east. A range of mountains towered above them, huge and sinister in the dark, and a coyote set up his yell. The salt-caked floor of the valley had changed to clean sand and the mesquite trees rose up in thickets. The narrow trail that Selim followed turned into another and another until a path, broad and plain, led straight to a trampled hole, pawed deep in a grass-grown flat.

Selim nosed in and sipped, then he drank deeply and sighed, and Morgan awoke with a start. In his ears was the gurgle of water, the splash of horses pawing mud as they struggled into the hole below. He fought his way among them, saving the last muddy water for his wife and the white-faced child. Then, digging deeper, he let the horses drink their fill before he picketed them out for the night.

Beneath the shelter of a huge mesquite the little family slept, too weary even to think of the prowling Indian forms that had dogged their footsteps at dusk. Dawn found them still sleeping when, with a sudden rush of hoofs, Selim and Neysa burst upon them and a stampede of horses swept past. An Indian war whoop rent the air and two of the fillies were gone, before Morgan could leap to his feet. Selim stood beside him, tense and eager and trembling to go, and with a curse the man leaped on his back and went whirling down the wind after his foes.

Across the flats like a fury he bore down on the fleeing Indians, who scattered at his impetuous attack. His yellow mount seemed almost to fly as, striking the *playa* of a dry lake, he galloped down upon them with long strides. Then Morgan's pistol came out and at the first loud report an Indian warrior toppled from his horse. The two fillies were left behind, unnoticed, while the swift yellow stallion skimmed the lakebed like a swallow and the pistol spoke again. Another warrior, run down, went off into the dirt with a bullet hole through his back, then with a pitiless hate the black-bearded man turned and went whipping after the rest of the band.

For an hour, while the stolen fillies stood staring, Randolph Morgan chased and shot until the last of his enemies had disappeared in the haze. Then, with both pistols empty, he rode back to camp, his eyes wild with a stern, killing rage. Beaten and thwarted at every point, he had turned upon the Indians with the pent-up hate of a madman, and, as he looked back down the valley where the looted wagon train lay, he called a feud on all mankind.

For a year, striving always to lose himself in the wilderness, yet conscious of his enemies in pursuit, he had pressed on into the West until in desperation he had entered this Valley of Death. The men he had followed had perished ignobly, giving the valley its tragic name, and to the world he, too, was dead. He turned his eyes to a deep cañon in the range of mountains above him, mountains that towered like a wall in the solitude of the desert yet opened one knife-like fissure to his gaze.

As the sun like a ball of fire rose blazing above the mountain, a man and woman and child passed through the knife gash entrance to Tingahnee, the Valley of Caves. In the lead paced Selim, his nose to the ground, following the scent of the wary mountain sheep, and at the end of the trail he led the way to a boiling spring that bubbled up and was lost in the sand. Along the cañon walls were deep caves, their sides blackened by many fires, but never again would the renegade Shoshones use the grinding holes of Poch Tingahnee. Randolph Morgan had taken it for his own.

Never again, while he lived, would the Indian women come trooping to pick the mesquite beans from the trees. The Shoshone hunters would go elsewhere to kill their mountain sheep, for a devil had taken possession of Cave Cañon. He was seen on the high cliffs that overlooked Toógahboth, the Night Water, where the fugitives had camped—a tall man with a white beard, a man who waved his arms and cursed until they fled from Night Water, too.

Years passed and the high mountain where Randolph Morgan hid was called Enúpi Kai, Devil's Mountain. In the shadow of the gateway that led up to the boiling spring, where before the Shoshones had camped, there lingered a presence that leaped out at them yelling and chased them across the flats. It was the devil in the form of a man, and they shunned the whole valley below.

At Esahbwoó, where the white people had been poisoned and died, the heavy wagons warped to pieces in the parching desert air and were buried beneath the sands. Nothing remained to tell the story of how they had met their death and no more wagon trains came that way—only prospectors, seeking gold, and outlaws with stolen horses, and fugitives who looked behind as they fled. Mines were found, and men rushed in, but they closed down and the miners left, and once more the Valley of Death lay, silent and empty, while the winds blew the sand to and fro, to and fro eternally.

Then an Indian, traveling at night, stopped at Toógahboth for water, and on the *playa* of the dry lake he beheld four golden horses, running and playing together in the moonlight. They were horses such as no one had ever seen before, with slender legs and high-crested necks, and they ran as no earthly horses can run. Their speed was like an arrow and in the morning, when they had vanished, there were no tracks on the smooth lakebed. But the old men remembered the white man with the beard—and the number of his horses was four.

A horse hunter from Nevada came and camped at Night Water, for the fame of the ghost horses had spread, but only wild burros wandered into his trap, and he rode away in disgust. Many years passed by before the horses were seen again, racing and gamboling by the light of the moon. But when the white men came, they found nothing but burros—only Indians could see the golden horses of Toógahboth. They ran too fast for earthly steeds—and, when the moon was bright, a ghost maiden rode with them, back and forth across the lake.

She was of more than mortal beauty, with golden hair like the horses' manes, and, when they played on the smooth *playa*, she leaped from horse to horse—and with her ran two sacred foxes. They leaped up at the horses' heads and all played together, until suddenly in the moonlight they vanished from sight and no one could find even a track. Horse hunters lay in wait, but the ghostly steeds avoided them, until at last only the Indians kept the story alive of the moon maiden and her magic mounts. So for twenty years they played and never felt the catch rope—and then Johnny Lightfoot came.

Chapter Three

The twenty years brought their changes, not all for the best, but the country to the east settled up. At Mormon Lake, over the mountains from Death Valley, a store and saloon had been built. A cold, wintry wind, springing up with the dawn, rattled the slats on Bodie's Bar, and four gaunt ponies, tied fast to the horse rack, bowed their heads to meet the blast. The sore-eyed Indian dogs crept under the house, while, within, the guttering candles still burned on the table and the all-night poker game dragged on.

Huge and dominant, with bleak, blue eyes that followed every flip of a card, Val Bodie sat stripped to his undershirt and overalls, from the band of which a pistol butt peeped out. Sleeping or waking, no man in fifteen years had caught Bodie without his gun. He sat with his back to the wall.

Across the table, the mark of the wolf on his face, Hank Boots crouched down behind his hand and thrust out a stack of chips, while his lips drew back in a snarl.

"Win that," he said, "and I'll buy the drinks and quit. By gad, it's almost day."

He glanced at the window where a pale streak of light was struggling through the pane, and for a moment his eyes shifted to three forms on the floor, where his half-breed sons slept like the dead.

"Win that stack and you've got me broke," he added.

Val Bodie spread out his hand.

"You're broke, then," he answered. "But the drinks are on the house. Git up, boys . . . your daddy is skinned."

"Skinned is right," grumbled Boots as he rose to his full height and stretched his long, gangling arms.

"Well, you asked for it, didn't you?" spoke up Bodie sharply. "Better keep a civil tongue in your head."

"I asked to play a game," returned Boots with an evil smile. "But, hell . . . you always win."

"Of course I win," boasted Bodie. "I'm a man with a head. Never seen the yap yet that could beat me. Here, take a drink of this and get the cobwebs out of your brain, betting your pile on aces and tens."

He snorted contemptuously and *thumped* a bottle on the bar, and, as the three sullen half-breeds lined up for their drink, he looked them over intolerantly.

"Every man to his own trade," he said at last. "You boys drift now, and steal some more cows."

"You buy 'em!" retorted Big John Boots.

Bodie nodded insolently. "Sure," he said. "Every man to his trade. I buy 'em because I know how to sell 'em."

"You know how to stealum, too," muttered the half-breed.

Then Grif Boots took up the tale. He was tall and Indian black, with glittering eyes that mirrored a settled discontent, and he shifted the gun in his belt. "We ride long time," he complained. "What's use go stealum cows? Me lay down, go to sleep. Wake up broke ... what's use? Me go stealum cow ... myself."

"Yes, and you'll wake up in jail," answered Val Bodie shortly. "What you got to say about it, Pete?" He turned to the youngest Boots, a boy hardly grown but with a tough, reckless cast of countenance. "Everybody else is bellyaching. What've you got to say? You want to steal cows for yourself?"

"Nope. Stealum horses," responded Pete succinctly, and Bodie burst into a roar.

"That's a good one," he said, laughing. "Have another drink, kid ... you've got all the brains in the family. Have another one, boys, and let Pete do your thinking. I'm going out to feed my horse."

He set the bottle on the bar and strode out the door, and Hank Boots rolled his eyes at his sons. His glance swept the half-empty shelves and he reached over deftly and filched a sack of tobacco. Then, rolling a cigarette, he lounged out the door and sat down to smoke in the sun.

From a corral behind the store eager horses looked out and whinnied as Bodie threw down some hay, but after he had fed them, he turned to a closed shed and poured out a feed of grain. Boots watched him and grunted as with purposeful care he rubbed down a clean-limbed mare. Next to whiskey and women, Val Bodie loved a racehorse, and this mare, no matter how, had been brought from Missouri to gratify his craving for speed.

"How's that for a horse, boys?" he shouted boastfully as he led the strange mare down to drink. "She's a thoroughbred, I tell ye. Watch them legs when she steps! She cost me a heap of money."

He watched as with dainty grace she bowed her head to the tepid spring and snorted at the alkali smell.

"Oh, she's a lady," he said. "She's accustomed to the best. And the best ain't none too good for her. While you boys were away, I took her over to Pahrump and beat every racehorse in town. They've got some good ones over there now . . . them gamblers and saloonkeepers are taking in gold, hand over fist. But Fly run away from 'em as if they'd been staked and I came back with a roll."

He slapped his pocket significantly, but, as the Boots boys exchanged glances, he slapped again—at his six-shooter. They slumped back in baffled discontent. Valentine Bodie was rich—he always had money—but he had killed several men and had served, so it was said, with the Avenging Angels, or the Mormon Danites.

Hank Boots grunted again and went over to the Indian camp, set back among a grove of huge mesquites. His boys followed behind him, their guns heavy on their hips, their eyes searching the brush houses warily. As they sat down by the fire, the Paiutes gave them food, for Boots and his sons were their kin.

Smoke rose from the big adobe where Bodie lived with his squaw. Breakfast was served and the master came out. But now he carried a riding saddle and, with his half-grown boy behind him, he led Fly to the edge of the lake.

Mormon Lake it was called, in grim mockery of its dryness, for the clay lakebed was as dry and smooth as a pavement, as clean and hard-tamped as a racetrack. But as Bodie mounted his son and prepared to start him on his canter, there was a yell from the dog pack by the store, and the Indians rushed out to look. Over the trail from Death Valley a lone man came striding in, driving two burros heavily loaded with ore sacks.

Bodie made a run for the store.

"Boys," he announced to the apathetic Boots family, "here comes Frying-Pan George again. I thought you said he was dead?"

"Well, we figgered he was dead," defended Hank Boots lamely. "Follered his tracks plumb out into them sandhills. Last we seen they was running in circles."

"He fooled you, the old walloper," declared Val Bodie savagely. "Can't you fellers keep up with a crazy man? He's loco as hell, but he's got a mine somewhere, and this time you follow him to it. What the devil do I feed you for, and keep you in whiskey, if you can't turn a trick like that?"

Hank Boots rose up and squinted down as he surveyed old Frying-Pan George. The latter's long, white hair was wrapped up in a red bandanna, which was tucked up beneath his hat, and he stepped forward jauntily in his buckskin pants and moccasins, carrying a rifle across his arm. Two pistols hung on his hips, and at sight of his black beard the Paiutes broke for the hills.

"You'd better run!" he yelled after them. "I'll kill every one of you. I'll kill 'em all, the lice and the nits!" He waved his arms threateningly at the crowd.

"Yes, and he will," spoke up Hank Boots. "I know that old devil. He'll shoot down any man that trails him."

"Heh, scairt already!" jeered Bodie. "He don't look bad to me. Look at them sooty-black whiskers, where he's rubbed 'em with the bottom of a frying pan. He must have an eye out for squaws."

"He's got a woman, somewhere," spoke up Big John Boots. "Always takes home a lot of calico."

"Are you afraid of him, too?" demanded Bodie. "Can't you trail him, when he goes? Your old dad here is scairt of his shadow."

"What you pay me?" asked Big John bluntly.

Bodie grabbed him by the shoulder. "You take me to his mine and I'll make you rich," he hissed. "Git him drunk, if you can, but trail him. And humor him, boys. He's crazy. All I want now is a look into them sacks."

He laid aside his rifle, which he had grabbed from the store, and walked out to meet his visitor.

"Hello, there, George!" he hailed. "I thought you was dead. What you got in them ore sacks, George?"

Frying-Pan George halted his burros and stood glaring at Hank Boots, who peeled his lip back in a scared, wolfish snarl.

"So you're here," boomed out the prospector, "you and your half-Injun brats! You followed me when I left here before. But I warn you right now, the next time you do it, I'll shoot. A squawman more or less is nothing to me. So look out or I'll pot you, sure."

He ran his eyes over the crowd and turned back to Bodie, who was regarding him with a placating smile.

"I've got ore in those sacks, sir! Ore!" he roared. "Are you willing to pay a fair price?"

"I'll pay you well," promised the storekeeper eagerly. Without another word Frying-Pan George dumped his packs on the ground.

Bodie cut the first sack open greedily and grabbed out a chunk of ore.

"It's rotten with gold!" he exclaimed. "Where do you get all this metal, George?"

"Never mind," replied Frying-Pan bitingly. "All I wish is a price on my ore. Otherwise, I'll hit the trail for Pahrump."

"I'll give you six hundred dollars a sack," offered Bodie after a hasty inspection of the ore bags. "That's a whole lot of money, George."

"It's nothing," declared Frying-Pan, "compared to what the ore is worth. But what could I expect from a renegade Danite that makes his living by robbing prospectors?"

He whipped out a buckskin thong and began tying up the opened sacks, and Bodie snatched out another piece of ore.

"By grab, boys, that's rich!" he cried admiringly. "Richest gold ore I ever saw. What's the chance of getting some more, George? I'll give you a thousand dollars a sack for all you bring in. Come on, George, that's lo-ots of money."

"You ignorant fool!" burst out Frying-Pan indignantly, curling up the blackened ends of his beard. "What the devil do you know about money? I've handled more in one day than you've in a lifetime. I'll have you understand, sir, I'm a gentleman."

"Sure, sure!" agreed Bodie. "I've seen gentlemen before. And one thing . . . they never haggled about the price. It's nothing to you, anyway, more than to buy a little grub, and maybe some powder and calico."

"Well, take it!" snapped Frying-Pan. "And give me a few necessities, so I can quit this scurvy crew. But put my money in my hand first, before I darken your doorway . . . four thousand dollars in gold."

"I'll go get it," promised Bodie, sweating. "But what's your hurry, George? Long time me no see you. Come in and have a drink on the house. I've got a new barrel, of the best."

"I never drink," stated Frying-Pan, "except with friends. So count out my money and fill this bill of goods. Go away, sir!" he cried as he kicked at a dog.

He stood in the open, muttering angrily to himself as he scanned the low hills to the north, and the Paiutes from their hiding places gazed down at him in terror, while the Boots boys slinked back out of sight. Every Indian, in his presence, felt the imminence of sudden death, for his eyes were crazy with hate. He waited while Bodie brought his payment in gold and stowed his numerous purchases in sacks, but to all Bodie's remarks he returned a hostile stare, meanwhile muttering contemptuously in his beard.

The dogs circled him, far away, as if scenting his malevolence and his ever-willing readiness to kill. As he packed his burros to go, they turned their eyes to the northern pass and set up a wild, warning yell.

An Indian was topping the ridge, followed by two closely packed mules, and a white man who rode forward to take the lead, but Frying-Pan saw only the Indian.

"As I live!" he cursed. "A murdering Shoshone! I'd like to kill the last one in the world!"

He stood glaring as they dipped down among the trees, and Bodie spoke to him soothingly. "That's

Captain Jack," he said. "He lives with the Paiutes. And he's bringing in a white man that maybe wants to trade, so you'd better leave him alone."

But Frying-Pan stood erect, his gun ready to shoot, and Bodie shrugged his shoulders. Captain Jack was no friend of his. The thing that caught his eye was a horse that the stranger led, a creature so deformed that it was almost a humpback, with low withers and a huge, rounded rump. But on its back was a light, English riding pad, and Bodie looked the cowboy over shrewdly

He was a tall and slender youth, with black hair and keen, dark eyes and an air of the braggart's confidence. Yet from the excellence of his rigging and the way he sat his horse, it was evident that he knew his way around. He glanced back casually as Captain Jack ducked in behind him, but, although Frying-Pan George held his rifle fully upon him, he did not break his pace.

"Git away from that Injun!" shouted Frying-Pan harshly. "He's a cussed Shoshone and, by the gods, I'm going to kill him! They're nothing but a bunch of murderers!"

"That's all right"—the stranger smiled—"but don't you shoot the Indian. I've hired Captain Jack to take me to a gold mine, and he can't very well do it if he's dead."

"He's just luring you out into the desert, where he can kill you for your outfit!" charged Frying-Pan George vindictively. "I know the whole murderous breed!"

"All the same, you let him live," replied the cowboy evenly. "Because he's a damned good horse hunter to boot."

He turned to nod approvingly at the square-shouldered Shoshone, whose sun-blackened countenance had turned ashy, and Bodie stepped into the breach.

"Hello, Jack," he greeted, advancing close enough to Frying-Pan to strike up his gun barrel if necessary. "What the hell are you doing, back here? Old Eatum-Up Jake will kill you."

"Me bringum back Hiko man," explained Happy Jack brokenly. "Maybeso findum Breyfogle Mine."

"Find nothing!" snorted Bodie. "Them Shoshones will sure git you, for stealing Eatum-Up's gal."

He stepped up closer and spoke a few words to Jack.

"No," responded the Indian stubbornly. "Me no run. My boss, she heap brave man."

"That so?" inquired Bodie, glancing fleetingly at the stranger. "What name she got, Jack, hey?"

"Name Horse-Ketchum," answered Happy Jack proudly. "Ketchum wild horse . . . Sundown Lake."

"The-e hell!" Bodie laughed. "What you think of that, George? This *hombre* here is out ketching wild horses. He's got one already. Look at that!"

He jerked a derisive thumb toward the hump-backed led horse, and Frying-Pan set down his gun.

"Well," he observed, ignoring Captain Jack and studying the points of the horse, "that ain't the worst horse in the world. Did you find him running wild, my friend?"

"Sure did." Johnny Lightfoot nodded. Horse-Ketchum was his Indian name. "He's the pick of four hundred that I rounded up at Sundown Lake. No fooling . . . that horse can run!"

"Yes, and so can that dog!" scoffed Bodie, making a kick at an Indian cur. "Why, my Lord, stranger, what the devil do you mean, leading him 'round with that pad on his back?"

"I mean," came back Lightfoot, "that old High Behind here can outrun any horse in Nevada, for dollars, dimes, or doughnuts."

"You want a race?" barked Bodie.

"Suit yourself," answered Lightfoot lightly. "Only after I win, I don't want any dispute. The first man across the line gets the dough."

"What . . . with that horse?" Bodie laughed, putting his hands on his hips and walking around High Behind incredulously. "Well, if he ain't sired by Star Plug, out of Battle Axe, then I sure miss my guess."

"That's all right," returned Lightfoot. "I heard you had a fast mare, so I came down to match a race. Put up or shut up . . . here's nine hundred dollars that I won in Virginia City."

"You want to race me?" shrilled Bodie. "That scrub against Fly? Lemme see if that money is good!"

He snatched the ten-dollar bill that Lightfoot handed him and held it against the sun.

"You're on," he said. "For nine hundred dollars. And, George, I'm sure glad you didn't kill Captain Jack or you'd have beat me out of this stake."

Chapter Four

The broad *playa* of Mormon Lake was a racetrack *par excellence*—so perfect in its smooth hardness, with just a trace of give, that Nature could do no more. The horse that could trot out between the stakes of Bodie's straightaway and not break into a lope must be poor and spiritless, indeed, but when Johnny Lightfoot rode High Behind up to the scratch, the horse plodded along at a walk.

Val Bodie followed behind him, watching the action of his legs, the muscle-bound rise of his rump, and at the end he burst out laughing.

"Stranger," he said with a wink at his men and a knowing leer at Frying-Pan, "that animile is new in these parts. I've heerd of this here High Behind that inhabits the mountain fastnesses and leaps from crag to crag like a goat, but I've never seen him down on the plains. Now yonder is a sure enough horse." He waved his hand proudly at the dainty mare as she warmed up across the flat, but Lightfoot only grunted. "A genu-wine horse," Bodie affirmed, "and not a dee-formed goat. I'd sure like to double that bet."

"Don't be too damned confident," observed Frying-Pan George, squinting his eyes at the hump-backed horse. "That nag has got some points."

"Yes, and so has a billy goat," answered Bodie, rubbing it in. "All this one lacks is the horns. Why don't you bet some of your money if you think he's got a chance? Come on . . . make a flash . . . be a sport."

"I wouldn't bet on a scrub race . . . and a crooked one at that," Frying-Pan George responded scathingly.

"Then you, stranger," persisted Bodie, riding up beside Lightfoot. "Is that all the money you've got? Well, anything else . . . a nice pair of spurs. I'll lay you fifty dollars against your saddle."

Lightfoot shrugged thoughtfully and reached down into his pocket. But he brought his hand out empty.

"All I've got," he said at last, "is a little piece of rock that I won from a Virginia City barkeep. A piece of the original Breyfogle ore . . . it cost me three hundred dollars. I'll throw it in the hat for five."

"You have?" exclaimed Bodie eagerly, and turned to glance at Hank Boots. "Lemme see it," he demanded craftily. "How do you know it's the genuine Breyfogle?"

"Because this barkeeper bought it from Breyfogle himself when he came back out of Death Valley. He put it up for the drinks."

"Well, lemme see it," insisted Bodie. "And if I think it's worth the price, I'll. . . ."

"You win this race," said Lightfoot, "and the rock is yours. You lose and you don't get a look. I'm hunting for that mine myself."

"Hoo, hoo!" mocked the storekeeper. "Out looking for the Breyfogle, like all these other smart guys. Did you ever think, pardner, that if that mine was really here, some of us old-timers would've found it?"

"You can't find a mine by sitting around a saloon," observed Lightfoot oracularly.

Frying-Pan George laughed heartily. His early antipathy toward Captain Jack's protector had changed to a fatherly tolerance that almost verged upon approval.

"Well, I'll go you," agreed Bodie, "for five hundred dollars. But who's going to hold the stakes?"

"Give 'em to Jack," suggested Lightfoot. "He's seen the rock already." He brought it out, wrapped up in a handkerchief.

"No, I know that danged Injun," Bodie spoke up brutally. "Any buck that will steal a woman will steal the stakes . . . or anything else. Let's ask Mister Boots here to serve."

"You do," cut in Frying-Pan, "and you'll have a thoroughpaced scoundrel that stands in, hand and glove, with Val Bodie."

"Well, in that case"—Lightfoot grinned, handing over the rock—"I'll just ask you to be the stakeholder, my friend."

"Very well, sir"—beamed Frying-Pan—"and you have my word, as a gentleman, that no one shall see this ore. You're a new man in these parts, so I might as well tell you that you've fallen into a den of thieves. There isn't a man here that wouldn't kill you for your winnings, or hold out the stakes if you won. You can govern yourself accordingly."

"I'll just put this gun where I can find it, then," answered Lightfoot after a glance at Val Bodie and his gang. He tucked a pistol under his belt. Then, still smiling serenely, he dropped off his horse and began to rub down High Behind.

"Why don't you give him a little run and kinder warm him up?" suggested Bodie, after waiting around uneasily for the start.

"That ain't my system," responded Lightfoot shortly. "How far do you want to run?"

"Quarter mile," announced Bodie. "That's Fly's regular distance. And we'll start at the drop of the hat."

"Suits me," agreed Lightfoot. "The stake-holder is the judge and no fouls allowed. The first man across the line wins."

"See here!" demanded the storekeeper arrogantly. "What shenanigan are you up to, mister? Do you figure on fouling my mare? I'll just warn you, right now, you lay a hand or a whip on Fly and I'll fill you full of lead!"

"All right," agreed Lightfoot, "and the same goes for High Behind. So lay off . . . and keep away from that homestretch."

He handed his hat to Captain Jack, with some muttered instructions, and swung up on his hump-backed horse. The spiritless steed then broke into an effortless canter that made Bodie stop and stare. With his ewe neck craned and his head thrust awkwardly out, he looked more like a camel than a horse, but in some miraculous way he got over the ground.

Val Bodie made a grab for Pete.

"Git that burro down here," Val whispered, "and git him here quick. This son-of-a-goat can run."

Strange as it seemed in retrospect, every man there present suddenly realized that High Behind had speed. That great rump that so deformed him was a mountain of bulging muscles that made him bounce like a rubber ball. Lightfoot rode him down the track to the scratch, then back again, running, toward the finish, where Bodie and his minions stood staring.

"What's the idea," demanded Johnny, "in setting all these posts along the track? Why don't we have this race in the open?"

"Oh, them's jest to keep the Injuns off the track," the saloonkeeper answered glibly. "They're hell to crowd in on the finish."

"Well, don't you do it," warned Lightfoot, "or I'll ride plumb over you. I may look easy, but I'm here to win this race . . . so don't pull any crooked stuff whatever."

"The same to you, mister," answered Val Bodie insolently. "You act pretty fresh for a kid."

"I run my horse on the square," retorted Lightfoot, "and I'd advise you to do the same."

He turned his horse in his tracks and trotted off down the course, but, as he lined up at scratch, he saw Pete Boots on a burro, flogging recklessly out from the store. Frying-Pan George had his hat held high in the air, and Fly's jockey was whirling her trickily in an effort to beat the game. But the hat did not drop and the half-breed came jouncing back to where High Behind stood fretting.

Once more the hat went up and the next instant it dropped. Fly was caught fighting her head, and with a single mighty bound High Behind jumped out into the lead. Lightfoot bent low and shot his mount down the track at a pace that increased with every stride. The awkward, ewe-necked creature became suddenly transformed into a living embodiment of speed. His long hind legs propelled him like a giant kangaroo and with each sweeping hop he pulled away from the high-bred Fly as if she were only a scrub.

The half-breed boy pulled his whip and laid it across Fly's rump in a frantic tattoo of blows. But

High Behind raced on, a good four lengths ahead, and Lightfoot saw the money in his hat. Before him in a blur there rose the crowd at the finish, and the line of narrowing mesquite posts flitting past, and then, moving slowly, a burro shuffled out, dragging a heavy rope across his path.

It was the same big burro that he had seen galloping out as he lined up to start the race, and Lightfoot sensed a trap. The next instant he was into it, for Hank Boots had sprung out and laid hold of the dragging rope. The burro sat back obstinately at the tug of the rope, effectively blocking the track, and Fly was dashing up behind. If Johnny slowed down, she would pass him on the run—when the rope was opportunely dropped flat—and beat him out at the finish.

A shout of warning rose up and men rushed to seize the rope, while Bodie ran out, waving his arms. But although he waved, Johnny Lightfoot did not check his racer's speed—the first man across the line won. Straight at the balky burro he headed his mount, and Bodie dodged back just in time. High Behind broke his stride and gathered his feet like a rabbit. Then, with a high, graceful leap, he jumped clear over the burro and went pelting down the track to victory.

With one resistless tug Val Bodie and his gang snaked the burro back off the track, but their desperate ruse had failed and Fly came dashing in, a beaten and disheartened horse. High Behind had won the race—but could his master collect the stakes? Johnny Lightfoot reined back and drew his gun.

Chapter Five

There was a rush toward the stake-holder as Lightfoot turned back to claim the pile of money he had won. All cursing at once, Val Bodie and his gang had swarmed in to protest the race, and with his black hair flying Johnny Lightfoot split the wind to get in before the stakes were lost. Straight at the crowd he rode, and, as they scattered before his charge, he dropped off and stood, gun in hand.

"I claim that race!" he said, turning to Frying-Pan George. "You know the rules . . . the first man in!"

"That's right," agreed Frying-Pan, reaching down into his hat. "Here's your money . . . and here's your rock."

"Much obliged," mumbled Johnny, stuffing the stakes into his pocket as he faced the surly crowd. "And now, you dirty whelps, you can all go to the devil . . . and take your trick burro with you."

"That was just a little accident," explained Bodie briskly. "But there's one thing I want cleared up. A race is a race, and my nine hundred is gone. But I put up five hundred dollars against a rock I've never seen, and I claim you won it on nothing. It's all right for you to say that it's Breyfogle ore, but I'd just like to see that rock."

"You'll see nothing," declared Lightfoot, "because I told you at the start. . . ."

"Now, look here," broke in Bodie, "I'm a peaceable man, but, by the gods, this is going too far. Pulling a gun won't get you nowhere when you're talking to me. I've tamed worse men than you are. All I want is to know that you've got such a rock and that it's the genuine Breyfogle ore."

"That's right, and that's fair," spoke up Hank Boots from behind him. "And if it comes to a fight, count me in."

He stepped up beside his boss, and, as his sons lined up behind him, Lightfoot put up his gun.

"Well, hell," he grumbled, "I'm not hunting for trouble. But suppose I show you this rock . . . who's going to decide whether or not it's the genuine ore?"

"I can do that, gentlemen," broke in Frying-Pan pompously. "I'm familiar with the Breyfogle rock. But if once Val Bodie gets his hands on that specimen. . . ."

"Then take it," offered Johnny Lightfoot impulsively, handing over the knotted handkerchief.

Frying-Pan opened it grimly, shielding the ore in his fists as he gazed. For a moment he stood blinking, then, with a slow, strange smile, he wrapped it up in the cloth.

"Young man," he said, "that's the genuine Breyfogle. But you might as well go back where you came from. Because, gentlemen, I brought four sacks of that same, identical ore and sold it at the store this morning."

"Like hell you did!" jeered Bodie. And then with a lightning slap he knocked the handkerchief out of Frying-Pan's hand. But as Bodie stooped to snatch it up, Lightfoot stamped down on it, and Frying-Pan whipped out his guns.

"You keep back," he ordered, as Lightfoot

grabbed the rock and rammed it into his pocket. "Keep back, and listen to me. There's no use fighting over this Breyfogle ore, because I've had the mine staked for years. And another thing, gentlemen . . . remember what I told you. Don't any of you whelps try to follow me. I'll bore the first that does."

He backed off toward the store, a pistol in each hand, his eyes on the men who, like a pack of wolves, were resolute to pull him down. Val Bodie was in the lead, and behind him Hank Boots with his band of half-breed sons—and suddenly their craven fear was gone.

The Breyfogle Mine was the greatest treasure that Death Valley held hidden from mankind. The man who first discovered it had carried out enough ore to set the whole country gold mad. Expedition after expedition had started back under his leadership, but each time he approached the scene of his early sufferings, the madness that had possessed him returned. Taken captive by the Indians, he had wandered from place to place, until at last, finding the gold, he had used his shoes for canteens and fled barefooted across the desert. Leaving Death Valley at night, he had passed two high buttes, below which were three white spots, like springs. At Hole-in-the-Rock he had drunk and passed on, until at daylight, topping a pass, he had discovered the seep of water still known as Daylight Spring. There he put on his shoes and wandered far to the south and east, trailed for days by the curious Paiutes who struck him down at last for his huge "moccasins".

But the gold they did not take, and emigrants, passing by, found him wounded and out of his head. Nor could he say where he had got the ore. He maundered of hidden springs, of a partner killed by Indians, of himself taken captive and ridden like a horse by a band of renegade Shoshones.

He remembered the two buttes, set at the entrance to the cañon at whose head he had found Daylight Springs, and the three white spots, like the seep of alkali springs, which he had seen near their base from the peaks. But whence the gold had come, he could never tell, for the stone war club of a Paiute had knocked out of his head the one memory that men sought most.

Fifteen years and more had passed, and now at Bodie's Bar a flash of the elusive secret had been revealed. Two men, riding in, had brought, one a piece of the ore, another four sacks from its source. But whence came this gold that Frying-Pan George packed in to trade for supplies at the store? And were the two pieces of ore really the same? One mystery succeeded another, for no man at Mormon Lake had seen Lightfoot's rock. All they had was the word of a half-crazy prospector that his ore and the Breyfogle were identical. But Val Bodie had them both in his power.

Plodding out through the gap that led to Daylight Pass and the arid waste of Death Valley beyond, Frying-Pan George drove his burros with the load of powder and supplies for which he had bartered his gold. He was keen and wary now, with his rifle across his arm, looking back often and shouting shrill threats. But the road he must follow led off across a desert that stretched smoothly to Death Valley's rim. On that broad, level plain, with the greasewood so evenly spaced that it looked like a planted field, not even a jack rabbit could hide. And his burros were slow. George would keep. Bodie did not worry about him.

With his winnings in his pockets and Captain Jack behind, Lightfoot had swung off into the Pahrump trail that led to the east and south. But the open, barren desert offered no hiding place for him, and Val Bodie came hotly on his trail. Lightfoot looked back, and unsung the rifle that he carried beneath his knee, for trouble was no novelty to him. In fact, he rather sought it, as a moth seeks the flame—and so far his wings were unsinged.

"Go back!" he signed, placing a bullet in front of Bodie.

The bad man came to a halt. Then Bodie raised his hand in the peace sign, waved his fighting men back, and rode out across the flat for a talk.

"Now, here," he began, as they met in the open, "I can't stop to monkey around with a kid like you . . . I want to see that rock."

He had mounted a big roan, slung a gun belt around his waist and a rifle scabbard on his saddle. Down the trail behind him on their desert-toughened ponies Hank Boots and his sons sat watching them intently, ready to ride in if a battle sprang up. But Johnny Lightfoot did not flinch.

"Say," he mocked, "do you own this country? I've got a use for that specimen myself."

"Well, you try to find the Breyfogle . . . or let me ketch you trailing George . . . and I'll damned soon show you what's what! I may not own the country, but I come pretty near running it. And you give me a little more of your lip and I'll sure plant you where you won't grow."

"I was just going to say," went on Lightfoot imperturbably, "that I'm free, white, and twenty-one, and I'll do what I damned please."

"Yes, I've heard that before"—Bodie nodded— "from a damn' sight better fighting men than you are. But I happen to be in a hurry right now. How much do you want for that rock?"

"I've got all the money I need." Lightfoot grinned. "What do you think of old High Behind now?"

"I'll be riding him in a month," retorted Bodie, "soon as I get old George off my hands. He's a good horse and I need him. And while we're on the subject, what's that Injun, Captain Jack, been telling you? I knew danged well, the minute I seen him, he was bringing you in here either to hunt for the Breyfogle or to ketch them wild horses at Night Water."

"That's right." Johnny nodded again. "Horse catching is my business. What's the matter? Isn't this a free country?"

"Well," responded Bodie, "it is and it isn't. I reckon you've never been in here before. Ever hear of Bodie's Danites? It's jest a name, of course . . . nothing to do with the Mormon church . . . but at the same time it covers the case. There ain't much of this country that ain't looked after by some of my riders, and we generally work by night. Kind of night riders, you savvy, and our principal occupation is looking after *hombres* like you. Sometimes we treat 'em easy, like I'm treating you now, and then again, my friend, we treat 'em rough as hell and bury 'em out in some dry wash."

"Yes, I've heard about that," admitted Lightfoot defiantly. "But, Mister Bodie, you don't look bad to me. And that goes for those half-breeds, too. I've trimmed you on a horse race and got away with the boodle, and I believe I can do the same with the Breyfogle. That is, if I happen to find it. But I've heard a whole lot about those Death Valley horses and you can't bluff me out. I'm going."

"You go," blustered Bodie, "and I'll see that you don't come back! There's no law in this country . . . no sheriffs, no nothing . . . and what Valentine Bodie says, goes. Them horses are mine. I've been over and seen 'em and I claim 'em by right of discovery. I sent plumb back to Missouri to get a horse fast enough to ketch 'em . . . that's how come I happen to have Fly. I've got Injuns on the look-out for horse hunters coming through there, with orders to smoke 'em out. And I'll promise you, right now, you'll never get off alive if you try to put a rope on my stock. Now that's doing a lot of explaining for a smart guy like you, that ought to be handled with a club, but, as I said before, I'm too busy to monkey with you and so I'm warning you out. Hit that trail there and keep a-going . . . and don't you come back, because I don't want you around here at all."

Bodie paused and regarded Lightfoot with a pair of steel-gray eyes that were cold and murderously calm, eyes that opened unpleasantly, showing too much of the white, eyes that had gazed on dead men and smiled. He was a natural-born killer, but Johnny Lightfoot was young and answered the threats with a smile.

"Well, that's plain, Mister Bodie," he said. "And next time I see you coming, I'll know just exactly what to do. The only trouble is . . . I'm not used to taking orders from a potbellied squawman like you. This is a free country, by grab! Or if it ain't, I'll make it free! And meanwhile, *you* hit that trail!"

He jerked his thumb toward the road that led back to Mormon Lake, and Bodie eyed him dourly.

"All right, mister," he answered. "I was going back, anyhow, so you can take your hand off of that gun. And don't you never think I'm bluffed. I've got other business on hand . . . trailing Frying-Pan George. And meanwhile you hit the trail. Understand?"

He wheeled his horse with a savage jerk and galloped back toward his men, while Johnny Lightfoot regarded him thoughtfully.

Chapter Six

From the top of a high butte on the Pahrump trail, Johnny Lightfoot, the horse catcher, watched five far-away horsemen riding out toward Daylight Pass. Ahead of them, like a shadow on the face of the desert, he saw through his glasses two burros that plodded west, flogged on by a black-bearded man. The latter went down to Death Valley and the five horsemen suddenly leaped into a lope.

"Come on, Jack," said Lightfoot. "I've got cards in this game. Maybeso we find the Breyfogle Mine."

"Nope . . . no findum," grunted Captain Jack, his keen eyes still following the chase. "Frying-Pan . . . she crazy. You think she ketchum mine? No good. Me trailum long time."

Lightfoot laughed at the badly mixed pronouns, but his eyes lighted up at the news. "Oho!" he exclaimed. "So you've backtracked George yourself, eh?"

"Long time, me trailum. She shoot like hell. No go to mine . . . turn back like fox. Every time Injun come . . . she shootum. Then long time me wait . . . see George going back. Two burros . . . plenty gold, like now." He stopped and chuckled, his strong teeth flashing white against the sunburned blackness of his skin. "Me follow tracks back," he said. "Findum hole . . . no gold! Frying-Pan stealum gold, then buryum. Bimeby she come back, digum up, tell Bodie ketchum mine."

"I see." Lightfoot nodded. "But where does he get this ore, then? Maybe you and me can steal a little, too."

"No-o. No good," returned Captain Jack soberly, rubbing a bullet mark on his neck. "More better ketchum horse."

"What horse?" inquired Lightfoot absently.

"Wild horse," said Captain Jack. "Good horse . . . kinder yeller. You think High Behind good horse? You think Fly horse run fast? No *wano* . . . me show you good horse."

"In Death Valley?" demanded Lightfoot eagerly.

The Shoshone nodded knowingly. "Death Valley . . . upper end. Long time Val Bodie try ketchum."

"*Umm*," mumbled Lightfoot—or Horse-Ketchum—polishing his gun butt dubiously. "Ain't you scared Bodie will kill us?"

"Maybeso we kill him," suggested Captain Jack, his crafty eyes gleaming wickedly. "These Shoshone horse . . . no b'long Val Bodie. Death Valley, Shoshone country. This side them mountains, all Paiute country . . . savvy? Other side, all belong Shoshone."

"Yes, but how about that girl you stole from Eatum-Up Jake? Bodie says the Shoshones will kill you."

"Nope. No stealum . . . run away," defended Captain Jack angrily. "Then pretty soon he marry white man. Me no stealum girl. Me good Injun, savvy? You let Shoshone kill me?"

"No, by grab!" declared Horse-Ketchum.

Suddenly Captain Jack smiled. "You good man," he said. "My friend. You no let nobody kill me, eh? All right ... me brave man, big warrior. You come ... me show you horse."

"That's a go!" exclaimed Lightfoot, holding out his hand.

Captain Jack shook it briefly. "Me show you good horse," he stated. "Too good, these horse. Nobody can ketchum. Maybeso spirit horse ... run fast."

"Let 'em run," boasted Lightfoot. "If I can't ketch 'em with High Behind, I'll give you a hundred dollars."

"*Wano!* Good!" Captain Jack laughed. "Me buy me 'nother squaw. These horse come nighttime. No likeum sun. You think you ketchum ... moonlight?"

"You bet." Johnny Lightfoot nodded. "Ketchum any time."

"Pretty horse!" praised Jack, rolling his eyes ecstatically. "Yeller horse ... come play on dry lake. Me watchum long time ... ride out ... try ropum. No good ... run fast, like that...." He clipped one hand across the other in the Indian sign for speed.

Lightfoot jerked out his roll of money. "Jack," he said, "you put me and High Behind where we can get a straight run at them horses, and I'll give you two hundred dollars. I got plenty ... two hundred dollars!"

"Good. Good," agreed Captain Jack. "Me buy me two squaw." He laughed as he brought up Johnny Lightfoot's horse. "You see moon?" Jack asked, pointing up at a pale crescent in the sky. "Bimeby come down there, get big. Come full moon, me show you horse."

"All right, then," replied Lightfoot. "Where you want to go now, Jack? Maybeso Val Bodie kill me."

"Nope. No killum," promised Captain Jack. "We go long ways . . . come back. Go Death Valley . . . come back. Val Bodie no seeum, no killum."

"Yes, good enough," agreed Lightfoot. As he fell in behind, he looked back at Mormon Lake and laughed.

The moon, which was on the wane, rose later and later, to float, pale and wan, through the sky, until at last it hung at dusk, crystal clear in the west—a new moon that grew and grew. The next evening it hung higher, an hour above the horizon, and so, night by night, until it rose in the east, huge and yellow, in the last rays of the sun.

For two weeks and more they had wandered through desert ranges, losing their tracks on the beds of dry lakes. But as the moon soared high, turning the color of gold, Captain Jack swung back into the north. Traveling trails that only his people knew, he headed toward the valley of Timbooshah, and Johnny Lightfoot found himself lost. Mountains rose where he expected valleys until at last, mounting a divide, he sensed the great abyss.

They stood at Daylight Pass, and below them, lost in moonlight, Death Valley seemed to shimmer and breathe. It lay before them, that mighty chasm where the earth had been rent and then half healed of its wound. A warm wind came to meet them as they descended into the depths, until suddenly at a black point the great sink appeared, its salt marshes gleaming in the moonlight. The Indian had wrapped himself in the mantle of silence, and the horse catcher held his peace.

They had entered unawares into an enemy country, where every man's hand was against them. Wandering Paiute or vengeful Shoshone or the night riders of Val Bodie would alike take up their trail. When, on the floor of the valley, they encountered the first sandhills, Captain Jack lost his tracks in the dunes. Then, as the mountains to the west cast their moon shadow upon them, he turned and rode to the north.

Rocky washes and wide expanses of salt meadow, where the crusted earth glistened with alkali, crossed their path. Then huge sandhills, studded with mesquite trees, rose up from the gathering darkness, and they struggled through a chaos of dunes. The moon had sunk from sight behind the ramparts of the Panamints, and in the east, above mountains that rose like a wall, there glowed the first light of dawn. They came out on a dry lakebed and before them; like fleeting shadows, strange creatures wheeled and fled into the night.

"Toógahboth," muttered the Indian as he reined in his horse. And for a long time they listened in silence to the patter of retreating hoofs. Then, down the wind, there came a loud whistling snort and Johnny Lightfoot's heart leaped with joy. Unseen by friend or foe he had reached the forbidden Night Water, and the golden horses were there.

Chapter Seven

At dawn, while their horses drank deeply from the water hole, Captain Jack circled the spring, his head low like a hunting dog's as he read the story written in the sand. Like a guiding automaton his forefinger swung here and there, lingering briefly as he studied out each track—until at last he came to a stop. Daintily stamped in the wet soil was the hoof print of a horse, round and firm and exquisitely formed.

"Yeller horse," he explained, as Johnny Lightfoot came, and then he pointed again. Half trampled by other tracks but stabbed deeply into the dirt was the mark of an iron-shod hoof.

"Val Bodie," the Indian said.

Lightfoot nodded. His enemy had been there, and gone.

"This bad place," observed Jack uneasily. "Injun devil watchum, too. She live up there, on mountain. Callum Enúpi Kai . . . my people."

He fixed his beady eyes on the forbidding cliffs of Devil's Mountain, and for a long time scanned them intently. Then he drew back closer behind the shelter of the trees and hastened to lead the animals out of sight. He bored deeper into the thicket of thorny mesquites that flanked the dry lakebed on the west, and, when all were safely hidden, he crept to a brushy hillock and once more gazed up at the cliffs.

They rose like the battlements of some medieval castle, their striated walls painted black and iron-red, or flecked with strange yellows and chromes. Behind them, deep in shadow, Lightfoot could see a cañon, cut out of the mountain's heart. Only the gash of a narrow gateway made its presence believable, and the wide, sluicing flow of the sand wash where cloudbursts had belched forth their waste. It was a place easily peopled by the savage imagination with demons that rushed forth to kill.

"Injun devil live up there," croaked Captain Jack at last. "We no lightum fire . . . she come down . . . maybe killum. Long time ago killum plenty Shoshones. My people no come here no more."

"What look like, this devil?" inquired Horse-Ketchum indulgently as he trained his powerful glasses on the cliff. "And, say, Jack, where are all those horses?"

"All gone," responded the Indian solemnly. "Maybeso moon takum. Yeller horse only come at night. One time me hide here . . . see spirit woman ride horse. Me think he drivum away."

"Maybeso," agreed Horse-Ketchum. "Injuns see lots of spirits, eh? You ever see this devil man, Jack?"

"Me seeum," asserted Captain Jack positively. "Tall man, long hair. Long whiskers, all white. She see us, she come down . . . killum. You look long time, topside big cañon mouth. Maybeso you seeum, too."

Lightfoot shifted his glasses to the crags above the gateway, but the great shelves and benches were empty and lifeless, without even a mountain sheep. There was not a tree or bush from the summit of the mountain to the base of the sun-blackened cliffs. All was barren, deserted, and yet, as he gazed, he, too, peopled the mountain with ghosts. From the shadow of a rock something rose up and slipped away—perhaps a man or a sheep or a light specter caused by heat, which was making the desert bushes dance.

The sun was over the peaks, pulling them out into strange shapes, distorting the broad valley that lay to the south until it shimmered in the semblance of a lake. As the sand absorbed its rays, the mesquite trees seemed to rise, as if floating away into space. Their gnarly tops were pulled up high— the mirage made them islands and their trunks became long, trembling stems.

Lightfoot crawled up again when the sun was smiting hot and trained his glasses on the demon-haunted crags, but only an Indian's eyes could see the man devil, gazing out over his desert domain.

In the breathless silence of midday the valley lay sleeping beneath its blanket of palpitating heat, but as the sun touched the peaks, a wind came stealing in, stirring the tops of the limp mesquites. Far away across the flats, where they had been grazing on the sacaton, a line of wild burros headed back toward the water hole, plodding slowly as if in a muse. But not a horse was in sight and Lightfoot became restless, for he did not believe in ghosts.

If the golden horses of Toógahboth came down at night to drink, and to gambol and play on the lakebed, his white man's reason told him that they did not come from the moon but from somewhere in that broad expanse. Before the dawn he had heard them as they pattered across the *playa*, and the wild, whistling snort of the stallion, but at daylight they were gone, as if, indeed, some ghostly maiden had driven them home to the moon.

At dusk they watered their animals and turned them out to browse on the leaves and beans of the mesquites, while from his pack Lightfoot measured out a feed of grain and fed it to High Behind. Then, as darkness came on, he rubbed him down and cinched on the saddle and limbered up his throw rope for the chase. When the moon rose over the mountain, like a globe of sun-kissed gold, he was waiting on the edge of the lake.

Down the wind there came the bedlam of wild asses braying and the rush of contending jacks as they fought. Then the burros came trooping in, to gather by the water hole and descend one by one for a drink. Pawing the sand back night by night they had dug a trench so deep that only their rumps remained in sight. Lightfoot thrilled at the thought of some glorious, golden horse, placidly drinking while he made his rush. But the horses of the moon did not come.

Higher and higher it soared, into a sky where the stars faded to nothing before its effulgence. Every tree and twig stood out, and the white *playa* of the lake stretched before him as clear as day. But it was empty except for the last of the burros as they plodded toward the salt flats to feed. Lightfoot felt his senses reel in a species of moon madness as he gazed out over the scene. Upon a night like that he could almost believe in moon maidens and flying steeds that no man could rope. But if any horses appeared, he was determined to ride out at them and match High Behind's speed against theirs.

There was a whistle, from far away toward Enúpi

Kai where the devil lay watching for his prey, and Lightfoot tightened up his cinch. Then, as High Behind raised his head and snorted back the challenge, Johnny reached up and grabbed his nose. Not six months before, on the *playa* of Sundown Lake, he, too, had run free, rejoicing in his speed, until at last he had felt the rope. He was a wild horse still, and only the stout hackamore held him back from a dash into their midst.

They came pattering across the lake, dim forms that glided near as easily as if they rode on a moonbeam. Lightfoot could see their heads as they flung them on high to sniff at the tainted wind. But he had placed himself well where no scent of his could reach them, and the horses, still snorting, came on. He caught the lines of a crested neck, a small head, and a short, straight back as the leading stallion circled close. Then, with a shrill, explosive snort, he turned and scampered off, golden yellow in the light of the moon.

Johnny Lightfoot hid, twisting the hackamore on High Behind to choke off his answering neighs, and, as he saw once more the tossing heads coming close, he turned and swung up on his mount. Man and horse alike were trembling now—the horse with eagerness to dash out and join his kind, his rider at the beauty of his prizes. Every line of their trim bodies spoke of symmetry and speed, and their tails, floating behind, stood out straight as tufted arrows. They came galloping, fleet as the wind.

Yet some instinct had taught them to avoid the crescent of trees that surrounded the lake and spring, and, as he set himself to go, Lightfoot felt misgivings. For the first time he doubted High

Behind's speed. Fastest of all wild horses at Sundown Lake, faster even than the thoroughbred Fly, there was something about the action of these swift, dashing mustangs that told Lightfoot his steed would fail. The horse band went thundering past him, their manes and tails like wind-tossed plumes, and he drew back, swearing, to wait.

In the open by the water hole the circling mustangs came to a halt while a beautiful mare, their leader, stepped out from the rest. Lightfoot counted seven more. Eight horses, so clean and perfect that each seemed a replica—and all yellow as gold in the moonlight. She advanced, sniffing the air, turning her head to right and left as if she sensed the hidden horsemen in the brush. But no one dashed out and she stepped down into the trench, bowing her head to the water in the depths.

The others crowded closer, eager to slake their all-day thirst but uneasy within the circle of the trees. Lightfoot made a move to charge out among them, but thought better of it while yet there was time. Once filled up with water, their speed would be cut down by enough, perhaps, to make one his prey. But even when the stallion ventured down into the pit, Lightfoot did not shake out his rope. Now, while that proud head was hidden, was the time to make his charge, to stampede the herd and capture the leader himself. But Lightfoot had lost his nerve. Something told him that to start was to fail, and he let the golden moment pass.

The stallion backed out swiftly, throwing his head into the air, then in a senseless stampede, playing and snapping as they ran, the horses sped out across the lakebed. Far off to the east they galloped, and Lightfoot thought they were lost until

suddenly he heard their swift hoofs returning. Yet
now there was a difference, coming subtly to his
ear that was trained to measure such cadences—it
seemed as if one of them was ridden.

They loomed up, dim and ghostly in the moonlight that veiled them with a soft, effulgent glow,
and now, a solid troop, they thundered by like
charging soldiers and Lightfoot saw the leader
wheel and guide. Then, as they swung in behind
him, Lightfoot beheld a woman's form, leaning forward along his neck as she rode. Her hair mingled
with his mane, her body seemed part of his, until
suddenly she rose up, revealing a face, white and
ghostly, and golden hair that flowed out behind.
Then in a *clatter* of hoof beats she was gone.

Johnny Lightfoot rubbed his eyes and stared up
at the moon, but the memory of that girl's face remained. Then again the hoof beats came and he
gazed out, incredulously, for the ghost woman was
riding, straight up. She rode bareback, graceful
and slender, on a mare that caracoled as gently as
any in a circus, and, as the stallion came rushing
past, she leaped lightly upon his back, seizing his
mane with a swift, triumphant swing. They were
off in a galloping circle, leaving the others far behind, and like a man in a dream Lightfoot watched
their prankish play.

But now, running beside her, were two silver-
gray foxes, the black tips of their tails whipping
about in the wind as they glided, unseen, over the
ground. Except for their black tips they were gray
shadows on a gray lakebed, but, as they dashed
into the lead, they leaped up at the stallion's head,
like dogs inviting their master to play.

Johnny Lightfoot sat rigid, his useless rope still

in his hand, and let the shadowy racers dart by. Here were horses, his eyes told him—the finest in the world—and a woman, more beautiful than he had dreamed. But whence came these foxes, to run and play at the stallion's head? And where had they suddenly gone? He strained his eyes to pierce the darkness, which no moonlight could quite dispel, and in the distance, moving together, he saw them gallop away until suddenly the night swallowed them up. With a curse he hurled his coil of rope to the ground and turned to find Captain Jack beside him.

"Somebody come," Jack stated stolidly, pointing off to the south.

Lightfoot came back to earth. While he, in a sort of dream, had watched the horses on the lake, Captain Jack, ever vigilant, had been searching the night for enemies—for at Night Water no man was their friend.

They took cover, and a single horseman came trotting out on the *playa*, as if driving the golden horses into a trap. Suddenly, from the east, a loud yell rent the air and in a stampede the horse herd came back. They were running wildly now, straight out across the lakebed where nothing could impede their flight, and behind them in a half circle shadowy riders appeared, whipping and spurring to cut them off. The lone rider had checked his steed, and, as Johnny Lightfoot crouched, staring, Captain Jack spoke hoarsely in his ear.

"Val Bodie," he said. "Ridum Fly horse."

Even as he spoke, Bodie charged. Like an arrow the highbred mare shot out across the lakebed, while Bodie, big and burly, shook a loop out of his rope, leaning forward to make his throw. But the mustangs had seen him coming—they swerved sharply to the south, and in a wild *clatter* of hoofs they raced off through the night, leaving Bodie and his thoroughbred behind. Lightfoot laughed shortly as he witnessed his rival's defeat.

Then Captain Jack took command. "No ketchum," he said. "We go."

Lightfoot turned reluctantly away. "All right, Jack," he answered. "But bimeby we come back. And then I'll ketch me . . . one horse."

Chapter Eight

When the moon, yellow as gold, sank down in the west and the sun topped the mountains to the east, Johnny Lightfoot, still riding, gazed back into the valley where the horses of Toógahboth ran. Val Bodie on his thoroughbred had been left at the start—the horse did not live that could match the golden animals—and yet, as he gazed, he muttered again: "Someday I'll ketch me . . . one horse."

Would it be the regal stallion that the moon girl had seemed to ride, with a mane as yellow as her hair? Or the mare who led the race, when the cowboys came charging in and they fled in a wild stampede? Or the filly, as free as air, which had kept its mother's pace, its head and tail lined out straight? There were speed and grace and beauty—but every one possessed them. They were perfect—the finest horses in the world!

Lightfoot's mount was tiring, but Captain Jack spurred on, his dark face grim and set. The pack mules jerked their heads and lagged as they broke their trot, but the Indian lashed them on ruthlessly. He did not look back, for he knew they would be followed as soon as daylight revealed their tracks. Val Bodie had promised to send them both to hell, and his night riders would try to make good.

At noon, from the black peak that guarded a hot spring, they saw the dust of the distant pursuit, and Captain Jack lightened his packs. Lightfoot changed to High Behind, and they turned off up a side cañon that led to the high plains beyond. All day, without pursuers, they fled on to the east, crossing the Grapevine Mountains and still pressing on until they came to a small, dry lake.

"Me foolum," promised Jack, riding out on its polished surface. After losing his tracks in circles, he turned to the south, doubling back toward Mormon Lake. Not till daylight, if then, would the weary avengers find the cleverly hidden trail they had made. By then more dry lakebeds would conceal their bold flight, straight back into the lion's den. Only when a pack mule quit and lay down beneath the lash did the Shoshone seek shelter and camp.

All day they lay in hiding, and the next night, beneath the moon, they circled until they passed Mormon Lake. Then, tirelessly, night after night, Captain Jack lost his trail and rode on, to lose it again.

"Me foolum," he said, grinning, and Lightfoot nodded.

So the moon waxed, and waned. But as it soared once more toward its throne in the east, whence soon it would emerge a full moon, and, as it lighted up the dry lakes with unearthly splendor, Johnny Lightfoot returned to his dream. On the *playa* of Toógahboth he saw the horses of the moon, trooping in to slake their thirst at the spring. He saw the stallion, his head erect, his golden mane gleaming, circling the flat while he whistled his alarm. Then the mare, her slender legs all set to wheel and run, walked in on the pawed-out hole.

He saw them drink and scamper away, rejoicing in their speed, challenging the horse hunters to do their worst. Behind them, on his thoroughbred, the fat and burly Bodie, laid the rope across Fly's rump in sheer chagrin. He was a rough man, a hard man, and he had those in his gang who would not hesitate to kill if they could. But he was only a man, and the golden horses of Night Water belonged to the first one who came. They were wild horses, free to roam over the limitless sink, free to drink at twenty hidden springs, and the first man who could ride up on them and snare one with his rope could hold him against the world.

"Jack," announced Horse-Ketchum as he watched the half moon rise, "I want to go back . . . ketchum horse."

"Huh!" grunted the Indian. "Val Bodie . . . she kill you. How much you give me, I go?"

"How much you want?" countered the other eagerly.

But Captain Jack would not say.

"You afraid?" demanded Horse-Ketchum at last.

"No! No 'fraid nothing!" answered Jack valiantly. "You give me fi-ive hundred dollars . . . me go."

"Five hundred!" cried Lightfoot, not to yield too quickly. "That's a whole lot of money, Jack. Don't you know it's against the law for an Injun to get rich? What the hell do you want with all that?"

"Buyum wife," responded Captain Jack promptly.

But Horse-Ketchum shook his head.

"*Ump-umm*," he protested. "We've got troubles enough, already. Who'll help me ketch horses if you buy yourself a wife? All the time, you stay at home."

"Nope . . . five hundred dollars," repeated the Indian expectantly.

Horse-Ketchum slapped him on the back. "Say, who is this lady?" he bantered. "Another girl of Eatum-Up Jake's?"

"No. Good woman," stated Jack. "Maybeso Paiute girl. You give me five hundred . . . me go."

"And you don't give a damn whether Bodie gets you or not, eh? All right, Jack, come on. It's a go!"

Captain Jack turned his horse and headed north by the stars, and three nights later they rode into Night Water, where a horse trap had been built, and torn down. Only the solid posts remained, set deep around the trench where the mustangs went down to drink. Lightfoot and the Indian dismounted in the moonlight and sought long for human footprints. Val Bodie had built the fence and swung the huge gate—but who had torn it down?

"No *wano*," pronounced Captain Jack, slapping his leg emphatically. Instinctively he raised his eyes to where, black and menacing, Devil's Mountain towered above them like a wall. "No good," he said again. "Yeller horse all go 'way. Maybeso, devil man come here."

"Maybeso," agreed Lightfoot. "Where you think horses go? You don't reckon Val Bodie caught 'em?"

"Nope. No ketchum," decided Jack. " 'Nother spring . . . over here." He pointed toward the west.

They filed out across the flats, where the self-rising ground had puffed up and formed a hard crust, until at last a broader trail led them to a hidden hole, where the burros had pawed out fresh dirt.

"Yeller horse," observed the Indian, pointing eagerly to a track.

Once more Lightfoot saw the round, dainty hoof

marks, newly made in the trampled earth. But this water hole lay in the open, amid hummocks of coarse grass and surrounded by miles of the treacherous self-rising ground, where in a chase the best of horses might fall. "We'll shirt tail it," he decided.

Hanging rags on stakes and strings, they went back to Night Water, to lie in wait when the wild horses came in. For the same fear that had driven them to abandon their old watering place would now send them back to Toógahboth. A rag fluttering in the wind, the suspicious line of white string, carelessly stretched to surround the water hole, would conjure up visions of horse hunters in hiding—and the fence around Night Water was old.

Many times, since it had been set and then torn down to the bare stakes, the golden horses must have circled it while the stallion snorted and whistled and the lead mare sniffed from afar. But now, driven by thirst, they would come back more eagerly. The two left the water hole undisturbed.

All that day, making no smoke, they lay hidden among the mesquite trees, where their animals could browse and eat. But, although he waited for two whole nights, while the moon approached its full, only burros returned to the spring.

Captain Jack, torn with fear of the Indian devil of Enúpi Kai—who he considered the protector of the horses—and yet resolute to win his $500, lay hidden day and night on the summit of a huge hummock, where the sand had buried a mesquite tree to its tips. Crouched down behind the brush, he watched the cliffs with staring eyes, turning his head again and again to search the desert to the south for signs of Val Bodie and his band. There was danger on every side, but Johnny Lightfoot would not give up. That night the moon would be full.

"What's the matter, Jack?" Johnny asked as they saddled up at sundown. "Don't you know some other place where maybe these horses drink? You think, now . . . some other spring!"

"Maybeso Hole-in-Rock," responded Captain Jack at last. "Me go up there tonight . . . puttum rock over hole. Then horse come down here . . . you ketchum."

"Why, sure," agreed Johnny. "Why the hell didn't you say so, instead of waiting around for three days?"

"Me no likum Hole-in-Rock," explained Jack. "Val Bodie ketch me there . . . she kill me."

"I see." Lightfoot nodded. "Well, don't let him ketch you, then. But you run those horses down here, where I can get one more chance at them, and I'll give you your money. You can go."

"You gimme five hundred dollars?" demanded Captain Jack eagerly.

Lightfoot nodded grimly. "You bet," he assented. "But you find them horses, savvy? This is getting kind of spooky, and first thing we know Val Bodie is liable to drop in on us. Have you seen that old devil man today?"

"Me seeum," stated the Indian briefly. "You look out. Maybeso she kill you."

"Ye-es, she'll play hell . . . killing me," scoffed Horse-Ketchum. "I'll just plug the devil right where his suspenders cross, if he tries any rough stuff with me."

"You look out," warned Captain Jack, swinging

up into his saddle. "Tonight full moon . . . Injun devil makeum medicine. Maybeso Val Bodie makeum, too."

"I'll make a little myself, then," promised Light-foot. He slapped the worn holster of his gun.

As the sun sank in the west, a great light appeared, as if, behind the mountains to the east, the world itself was afire. The sky was lit up with a red-and-yellow glow, until at last over Devil's Mountain, like a ball of enameled gold, the moon rose up majestically. Every crater on its surface seemed to stand out like a pit hole, its huge ranges cast broad shadows across the plains, and the sun, scarcely hidden behind the rim of the world, made its sister of the night gleam like day.

Johnny Lightfoot cinched up High Behind and took his post behind a tree, but his eyes, which at first were wary and intent, soon grew big with the wonder of the scene. Devil's Mountain rose before him, its cañons deep and black, its high cliffs etched with lines of silvery light. On the *playa* of the dry lake mystic figures appeared as the wild burros paced in toward the spring. In the moon-light their runty bodies were transformed to ghostly horses, their huge ears to crested manes, and, running dimly among them, he seemed to see silvery foxes that leaped up to kiss their noses as they passed.

It was the old moon madness coming back. But when the burros stumped past Lightfoot to gather about the water hole, he laughed and shook out his rope. Let Jack see Indian devils, and maidens who rode by night on the backs of golden steeds—all he believed was what he saw, and not half of that. But this time there would be no delays. When the golden horses came, he would ride out and make his throw. He would tie to the phantom stallion and let his rope be the judge—if it passed through the horse, then all was a dream.

Scuffling and braying in clownish abandon, the burros drifted off, to graze on the coarse sacaton, and, keeping his long vigil, Lightfoot waited. He was fetched up by a shrill neigh from High Behind, a neigh that rose, eager and piercing, and ended in a snort as Johnny laid a hand on his nose.

All was silent then, and the broad, white lakebed brought back no answer to his call, but in a tremble of excitement Lightfoot tightened his cinch and whipped the kinks out of his rope. Then he listened, and at last down the wind there came a whistle that he knew. The golden stallion had returned.

Across the *playa* something moved, something that seemed to glide on air, but Lightfoot knew it was a band of wild horses, circling about before they came in to drink. They were tired, for they traveled at a walk. Weary miles lay behind them if they came from the spring where Jack had covered the hole with a stone. They were thirsty, and they broke into a trot.

Down the wind from the water hole, behind a barricade of sand drifted up against the body of a tree, Johnny stood watching in the blackest shade, twisting the hackamore on High Behind's nose. Man and horse were trembling now in anticipation of the chase, but Lightfoot's nerves were calm. He felt none of the indecision that had come over him before and held him back from the start—and yet he bided his time.

Weary and gaunted although they were, the golden horses could still outrun him. He waited until the mare, stepping forward out of the band, went down into the trench to drink. Then he mounted silently, although the stallion snuffed the wind, holding back while his *manada* went in.

With heavy sighs, one by one, they backed out of the trench and stood, drooping, while the others went down—yet Lightfoot withheld his hand. The golden stallion still stood guard, shying suspiciously at the circle of posts that had been set when Bodie had made his trap. Of all these glorious horses he was the noblest by far. Johnny Lightfoot waited—for him.

Sniffing the wind, sniffing the sand with its faint human taint, his head pivoting as he scanned the shadowy trees, he entered at last into the circle of deep-set stakes and glided down the incline to drink. Lightfoot shook his rope out, his lips murmuring a sort of prayer as the last slow seconds passed. He felt exalted, almost religious, raised above his common self by the thought of what lay before him. One careful, measured rush—a flip of the rope—and the golden stallion was his. The most beautiful horse in the world!

He rode out slowly, hanging low behind his horse, and for a moment the mustangs were deceived. They stood staring, their heads erect, their nostrils quivering in frightened snorts, and Lightfoot threw in the spurs. But, although High Behind leaped forward in a series of mighty strides, the wild horses galloped away—beyond the sweep of the rope, spurning the earth in a drumming stampede. Only the stallion, head down in the narrow trench, was left behind in the flight.

At the sudden rush of hoofs he backed out with a whistling snort. His wind-swept mane seemed to bristle as he faced the charging horseman. Then he whirled and dodged out between the posts of the half-wrecked trap, every muscle in furious action. The ground trembled beneath the impact of his racing hoofs, but High Behind was upon him, charging down in full stride, and Lightfoot shook out his loop.

The reata whistled in swift circles as he poised for the throw. Then, as the stallion straightened out into his swift, resistless pace, Lightfoot shot out his rope. They were running like the wind, but the plaited rawhide went straight and true. The long loop hovered and spread, and settled around his neck. The golden stallion was snared! Lightfoot took his dally and set High Behind up, leaning back to hold his saddle against the jerk. Then the stallion hit the rope and went tumbling, heels over head, and Johnny took up his slack.

Chapter Nine

Like a man who has angled for long in some pool when he feels the tug of an enormous, fighting trout, and sits back, playing him warily, so Johnny Lightfoot, the mustanger, thrilled all over at the jerk, and gave the golden stallion more rope. But the animal did not run against the slack, to hurl himself once more, thrown and sprawling, across the smooth sands. Somewhere before he had felt the bite of rope and he now came charging at his captor.

Lightfoot threw off his turns and reined quickly aside, holding his coiled rope high for a flip. Then, as the stallion wheeled and reared, his forehoofs raised to strike, a loop came spinning down the rope. It encircled the poised hoofs like the writhing of a snake and the stallion fell heavily to the ground. Another loop followed, drawing the forehoofs close together, and Lightfoot stepped down from his horse.

In his hand he held a *jáquima*, the rawhide hackamore of the horsebreaker—a heavy nose piece of plaited thongs, rigged with ropes to form a halter that, when pulled, would cut off the breath. Waving his hat at High Behind to make him keep the reata taut, Johnny went down the rope to where the stallion had fallen, and jumped, straddling, on his neck. Over his nose with a practiced jerk he slipped the breaking halter and adjusted it behind his ears. Then, with two ropes instead of one, he swung up on his mount and flipped off the binding loops.

The stallion came up snorting, and Lightfoot leaned back to meet the shock of another jerk. But somewhere this wild horse had learned the lesson of the rope, for now he did not run. He shook his head and looked around, every muscle trembling, then, facing the east, he neighed, long and shrill. But his *manada* did not respond. They had fled into the night—he was alone.

Lightfoot rose up closer, pulling gently on his hackamore, and suddenly the wild mustang was tame. He yielded to the tug before the cruel bosal closed down against his sensitive nose, and, when Lightfoot reined away, he followed after his captor obediently, yet always with his eyes to the east. Again and again, like a quavering cry for help, he let out his piercing neigh, until at last, from the night there came a distant answer, clear and high— the call of his mate.

Lightfoot leaned back and watched him, taking in with admiring eyes every line of his beautiful prize—the small, sensitive ears, the full eyes, the flaring nostrils, the proud set to his head as he neighed. Every part of him seemed perfect, for endurance or speed—the straight back, the slender legs, the heavy muscles of shoulder and hip. He had all the points of a thoroughbred, and yet Death Valley was his home. Johnny spoke to him softly, but now the stallion had turned and was gazing away to the south.

High Behind switched his ears and listened intently, his sensitive nose testing out the wind. Then he, too, gave a neigh, and soon across the lake Captain Jack rode up to them, laughing.

"Ketchum horse, hey?" he cried as he paused to survey the prize. "Me findum track at spring . . . put big rock on hole. Bimeby horse come . . . me driveum."

"Well, bully for you, Jack!" exclaimed Horse-Ketchum exultantly. And, whipping forth his pocketbook, he counted out $500 into the Indian's expectant hands. "Now," he went on, "let's get out of this country. Listen to that!" The stallion had neighed again.

"No *wano!*" warned Captain Jack. "You pullum rope, makeum stop. Injun devil, she come here sure."

"Val Bodie's the only devil that I'm afraid of," answered Horse-Ketchum. "What's the quickest way out . . . straight north?"

"Go Hole-in-Rock," responded Jack. "Ketchum water . . . hide all day. This horse, she fight like hell."

"No. No fight!" declared Horse-Ketchum. "Look here, how he leads." And he started slowly off across the dry lakebed.

"Too good, that horse," observed Captain Jack cynically. "You look out . . . maybeso she kill you."

"Kill me . . . nothing!" retorted Horse-Ketchum. "He's gentle, I tell you. Somebody else has caught him before."

"Maybeso somebody else ketch us," grumbled the Indian. And he loped off to pack up the mules.

They pulled out on the run, the golden stallion following free as they rode away across the dry lake, but, when they turned into the trail that led east to Hole-in-the-Rock, he set back and fought the rope.

"Yeah, she tame!" jeered Captain Jack, riding warily in behind him.

As Horse-Ketchum reined his mount to keep clear of the thrashing slack, Jack laid his quirt across the stallion's rump. The horse jumped forward, striving purposely to entangle his captor. Then, with teeth bare and gleaming, he charged back at the Indian, who promptly took to the brush.

"Leave him alone!" ordered Horse-Ketchum, after the flurry was over. And, setting back gently on the hackamore, he cut off the stallion's breath. Three times he pulled and slackened, and then with a great sigh the golden horse accepted his fate. At the tug of the rope he followed along obediently, but at every turn and corner he looked back. Up the smooth, hard streambed, laid down by some cloudburst, they swung along at a rapid trot—past the Breyfogle Buttes, past the looming point of rocks, and into the dark cañon beyond.

Hole-in-the-Rock lay before them, with its dim trail up to the spring, when suddenly, out of the darkness, they rode forth into bright moonlight, and with a snort the stallion began to buck. Out of the corner of his eye Lightfoot saw the pack mules, fleeing madly back down the gulch. He glimpsed Jack, whipping after them—and other forms that meant nothing as he clung to the saddle and rope.

High Behind was jumping in circles to keep the slack from under his hoofs, and Johnny was playing the bounding stallion like a fish, when from the blur of movement about him a rawhide rope came—*slap!*—and his arms were pinned to his sides. Another loop roped the stallion—they came pelting in like rain, and he found himself jerked to the ground. Then, as his head ceased to spin, he saw horsemen all about him, and Val Bodie looking down at him, laughing.

"I got ye, eh?" he taunted, swinging down from his horse and snatching Johnny's gun from its holster. "Red-handed, by grab! But I'll have to admit it . . . you're the most accommodating and obliging son-of-a-bitch that I've met with in many a day. You not only ketch my horse, but you bring him right to me!" He leaned back, shaking with laughter.

"And he got the stud, too!" shouted Hank Boots triumphantly. "The best danged horse in the band. If that ain't being clever, what is?"

"One good turn deserves another." Bodie chuckled. "Just for that, boys, we'll let him live. Turn him loose, to rustle. Maybe next time we ketch him, he'll have us another fine horse." He glanced across admiringly at the stallion.

As Lightfoot felt the sting of their laughter, he fought against the ropes, cursing furiously. After all his hard riding, his weeks of danger and toil, he had ridden into the hands of his enemy. But he would not give up the horse.

"You leave him alone!" he shouted. "I caught him, and, by the gods, he's mine! You steal that horse and I'll come and steal him back. He's mine, I say . . . he's mine!"

"That'll do, now," warned Bodie, jabbing a gun against his ribs. "It's no trouble at all to throw a rope around your neck and drag you to death over the rocks. That's what I intended to do when I rode down to the spring and found where you'd covered up the water. That's a crime out on this desert . . . the worst crime of all. But nobody can say that Val Bodie ain't generous . . . and you've sure done me a good turn. With this stud here for bait, I can build me another trap and ketch every mare in that band. Now think this matter over and don't speak too hastily. Don't say anything that you're liable to regret. Didn't I understand you to say you was bringing me back this horse, being as I told you, once before, he was mine?"

He put up his pistol and dropped a loop over Lightfoot's head, and Johnny saw he was whipped.

"Well . . . take him," he answered sullenly.

"I'll do that," responded Bodie, "and thankee kindly, stranger. You're not such a fool as I thought. I was going to strip you clean and turn you loose on the desert with your hands tied behind you, barefoot. Now there's another little thing that I'd kinder like to have . . . as a memento, you might say, of our meeting. Something to remind me of you, when you're gone. You mentioned one time a piece of rock you had. I'd like that Breyfogle ore."

"What is this?" demanded Johnny. "A hold-up? Are you going to steal everything I've got?"

"No, not if you're reasonable," answered Bodie. "All I want is that piece of rock."

"And if I give it to you," bargained Lightfoot, "will you let me have my horse . . . to get out of this cursed country?"

"You can have old humpback," replied Bodie scornfully. "Only be damned sure you keep a-going. Don't let me ketch you back again, mixing up in my affairs and trying to find my mine. Because if I do, I'll beef you for a certainty."

"Take these ropes off," ordered Lightfoot fretfully.

When his hands were freed, he fetched out the precious specimen and handed it over to Bodie.

"Well and good," observed the saloonkeeper, looking it over by moonlight and thrusting it into his pocket. "Now I'll just take your carbine and pistol, so there won't be no argument about it. And yonder, up the cañon, is your road."

He flipped off the last reata and Johnny Lightfoot took the road. But at the turn of the cañon, he stopped. He was unarmed, but he was free, and somewhere in the hills Captain Jack would be watching for his smoke. Val Bodie had twenty men and they were only two, but Johnny had gazed upon the beauty of the moon horses and he reined High Behind back into the Valley of Death.

Chapter Ten

On the south flank of Breyfogle Butte, as the moon sank low, a fire flared up and died down suddenly, then leaped up with a fiercer glow. It winked out, and blazed forth again for as long as a desert greasewood could give off its feeble flame. At last, far down on the floor of Death Valley, an answering signal shot up. Two fires, side-by-side, and Johnny Lightfoot knew that Captain Jack had seen.

An hour later they came together in a rocky wash, Captain Jack hanging back and sending his pack animals ahead, for fear of another trap. He stepped out of a black shadow when he heard Horse-Ketchum's voice, but his old confidence was gone and he hung his head in silence, as if expecting a just rebuke. For at the first sign of danger he had whirled and fled as if the devil of the mountain were after him.

"Well, Jack," spoke up Lightfoot, "I reckon here's where you and I part. Val Bodie took my horse and I'm going back after him. All I want is some grub . . . and your gun."

"My gun?" repeated the Indian. "What for?"

"Never mind," answered Lightfoot. "Val Bodie took mine . . . and this one is no good to you, no-how. You take the outfit and wait for me at Pah-rump. Hurry up and open up that pack."

He stuffed a flour sack with jerked meat and a

little bread and coffee, then fished out his spare pistol from the bottom of a saddlebag and strapped it around his waist.

"Where you go now?" demanded Captain Jack gruffly. "Maybeso Val Bodie kill you."

"Well, he'll never get you," rejoined Horse-Ketchum sarcastically. "So come ahead ... gimme that gun. All you need is a pair of spurs when it comes to a fight. You're brave as hell, ain't you, Jack?"

"What for me git killed?" demanded Captain Jack indignantly. "Me seeum plenty men, all ride up at once. Me see horse buck. No can leadum away."

"Nope, I lost him," agreed Lightfoot. "But the show ain't over yet. Only I can't whip twenty men with one old six-shooter. So what about that one of yours?"

Captain Jack fingered ruefully the butt of his precious pistol, the symbol of his warrior's estate. But he had not made good on his oft-repeated boasts, and at last he unbuckled his belt.

"You takeum," he said. "Me wait for you ... Pahrump. Maybeso me no see you again."

"Don't you worry," responded Johnny Lightfoot grimly. "You've got five hundred dollars and all the time in the world. Now you stay there, savvy, until I come."

"All right," agreed Captain Jack, and turned the mules back into the hills, to make a dry camp for the day.

Lightfoot rode back north, straight for the Brey-fogle Buttes, and at daylight he crept out on a point and trained his glasses on Night Water. There were men there, cutting mesquite poles and setting posts around the spring where their water trap had been destroyed. Tied to a heavy stake for his mates to see, if they returned, the golden stallion stood drooping.

Lightfoot muttered to himself and scanned the desert floor, where in great reaches of gravel and broad alkali-whitened flats, Lost Valley stretched away into the haze. Here and there on the wide expanse he spied burros in twos and threes, grazing on salt grass or browsing on mesquite tips, but nowhere within the sweep of his field glasses could he pick up the golden herd. They had fled to some cañon in the distant mountains or quit the country for good.

All through the day Val Bodie's men worked on, until their horse pen and trap were complete. Then, as evening approached, they mounted and rode away, leaving the stallion to fret at his stake. Nothing stirred in the thicket of trees that lined the edge of the dry lake, and the horsemen rode back the way they came. Lightfoot had counted them— and he knew Bodie's horse. There were six men hiding by the trap.

Night came, and he crept back to where High Behind was hidden, and rode down to an alkali spring. As the moon came up, he moved in toward his magnet—the horse he had won, and lost. So brief had been the time of his joyous possession, so urgent the necessity to escape, that he had never laid a hand on that glorious head and neck, except to fasten a rope. Fighting his head and pulling back, the golden stallion had done his best to escape his inevitable fate. And then, while the battle for supremacy still raged, Val Bodie had captured them both. Not once had Horse-Ketchum stroked

his velvety nose or brushed back the flowing mane.
It was a fight, from the start, but even while they
struggled, his heart had gone out to his prize. The
stallion fought with a courage that knew no defeat,
yielding only to bide his time for another, more
reckless break to gain the freedom he loved. Yet
now he stood, anchored fast to a stake, to serve as a
lure for his mates.

From the far end of the dry lake, Lightfoot edged
in toward him, keeping back under cover of the
brush. He had circled Night Water, to come in
against the wind, which was blowing up strongly
from the south. The air was full of sand and out
across the *playa* dead sticks and wisps of grass
went flying past. It was a good night for a task as
desperate as his, for every limb and bush was on
the move. Even the moon was half obscured by the
smudge of rolling dust.

He crept up till he saw the stallion. A massive
snubbing post had been set before the spring and,
half hidden by brush, two wings had been con-
structed, leading into a pen behind. Then the build-
ers had ridden away, leaving the stallion for a lure.
Somewhere among the trees lurked the mustangers. Lightfoot came on warily, his eyes on the
thrashing branches that masked every movement
behind them. At any moment from that thicket Val
Bodie might charge out at him, and then the best
he could hope for was a running fight, with High
Behind out in front. He was a horse that had no
equal among the mounts of the night riders. Not
even Bodie's Fly could keep up with him on the
level, and across the rocky draws he was invinci-
ble. In no more time than it took to leap upon his
back, Johnny would be safe from his enemies' pur-

suit. And if they came on shooting, he would stand and shoot back, for nothing could possibly be gained by flight.

Johnny Lightfoot had come to steal back his horse, and all the long night lay before him. He took shelter behind a mesquite tree and watched. All day Bodie's riders had toiled hard, building the trap. The night before they had been in the saddle. What would be more natural, if no wild horses came, than for the hunters to fall asleep? Lightfoot kept on his feet, to fight off the sleep that came over him, and the moon swung up to its zenith.

The wind went down, leaving the air still and murky, and the stallion began to fight at his stake. He set back against the rope, trying the hackamore with all his strength, but it held and he quit with a grunt. His proud head drooped again and he stood patiently, waiting the next move in a losing game. Wild burros came trooping in, to snort their distrust as they gazed at the fenced-in hole, and suddenly the golden stallion pricked his ears to the east. He neighed, and there came an answering call.

The burros stood staring. Lightfoot tightened his cinch, and across the silvery lakebed a single horse trotted in—it was the lead mare, returning to her mate. Now the chance had come for which Lightfoot had waited. There would be mounting and riding, a chase across the *playa*—and, while Bodie and his riders sought to pen the faithful mare, the stallion would be left unguarded. Lightfoot backed deeper into the thicket, while out across the lake the mare came trotting, with her head up.

Johnny gazed at her covetously as, half revealed

by the dim moonlight, she circled and sniffed the wind. She wheeled and raced away, but soon she was back again, whickering softly to her captive mate. She advanced and set her hoofs, ready to whirl and run at the first sign of impending pursuit. But she came on, almost to him, and something in her gait suddenly caught Lightfoot's trained eye. She traveled like a horse that was ridden.

She whirled as if to flee, and above her floating mane Johnny saw a head bob up. It was the head of the moon maiden, lying closely to the golden mane that mingled with her own flowing hair. As the mare wheeled, snorting, he saw the form of the rider, clinging closely to her side like a bat. With a quick slap at her head she brought her mount up to the stake. Then suddenly she leaned down and cut the stallion's rope loose, and Lightfoot knew the rider was a woman.

Living with Indians so much and listening to their talk, Horse-Ketchum had come almost to believe in their stories of devils and ghosts. Almost, and not to oppose him, he had conceded to Captain Jack the presence of a devil on Enúpi Kai—a man devil who watched over the ghost horses. But, when his rope had snared its neck, the ghost stallion had proved real—and now the ghost maiden had flashed a knife.

She rose up triumphantly as the tie rope was slashed and headed the stallion back toward the hills. But as he jumped to escape, his forehoofs were jerked from under him and he fell sprawling— he was hobbled, to boot. Then a yell went up from a thin fringe of mesquite trees that extended out into the lake, and six riders came dashing forth.

Their ropes were swinging. They leaned forward against the wind, and their horses came on at a gallop.

The moon maiden turned to flee, then she dropped to the ground and ran back to the struggling horse. Like a flash the startled mare made a break to escape, but a rope brought her up with a jerk. The woman was stooping over to cut the stallion loose when a reata dropped over her head. Six riders with six ropes made their casts into the scramble, and every loop fell true.

"Well, my Gawd!" whooped Bodie as he set up his horse. "Look what I got, while the getting was good! A girl, and a damned pretty girl!"

He dropped down and grabbed her as she threw off the rope. There was a struggle and a woman's piercing scream. Then Johnny Lightfoot, forgetting his mission, charged down on them, cursing. Val Bodie had the girl in his arms, struggling.

Chapter Eleven

A fiery rage had swept over Johnny Lightfoot at the first shriek of the moon maiden, who Bodie had roped as she fought. Johnny had come there to win back his horse, but he cast that thought aside and rode in on them, shooting furiously.

The horse hunters stampeded as if blown by a wind, carried away by the panic of their mounts, and, as Bodie saw the flash of a gun in his face, he ran without firing a shot. Lightfoot hurled one pistol after him and swung down by the struggling stallion, throwing the girl the rope of her mare.

"There's your horse . . . now ride!" he panted. He stooped down to cut loose the tangled stallion. He leaped in on him recklessly, feeling about for the rawhide hobbles, straightening up to get out his knife. Then, sitting on his neck, he slashed the hobbles loose and the stallion came to his feet. But as the horse plunged out into the night, Lightfoot grabbed the hackamore and sat back on the rope. They fought each other desperately, each intent on his own escape, but the man won, and Johnny swung up on High Behind with the halter rope wrapped around the horn.

For one instant, exultantly, he glanced back at the mesquite thicket where Bodie and his riders had fled. Then he turned toward the north, leaning forward against the tug as the stallion resisted the rope. Johnny's chance had come, and he had seized it. Now the stallion was his, and the woman was already forgotten. He had scattered the mustangers and won back his prize, the glorious golden stallion of his dreams. He sank the spurs into High Behind at sight of a man running toward him, but as his mount plunged forward a shotgun blazed and he felt the burn of shot across his back. The gun belched again and High Behind fell to bucking—bucking and running and squealing with pain.

Lightfoot grabbed the horn, turning sidewise to dodge the rope that was towing the stallion behind, and they took off across the dry lake. High Behind's tail was clenched down, his rump was twisted sidewise as he shrank from the hurt of the shots, but angrily, bawling and lashing, he bucked out into the night while Lightfoot rode him, reeling. The grip of his knees had weakened, his hand was wet as he grasped the rope, but through the storm of whirling and bucking he kept his turns on the horn. The golden stallion was his!

They went galloping across the lakebed and out into the rocks where a great sand wash came down from the hills, and here Lightfoot suddenly learned why the stallion had been led so easily. He was following after his mate, the mare. She had come down from Devil's Mountain to seek him when he was caught, and now he was heading toward home. But High Behind, shrinking and sidewinding from the burn of the buckshot, climbed the cutbank and headed north. As they started to leave the wash, the golden stallion set back, jerking the saddle until it slipped.

For an instant Lightfoot clung desperately with his spurs, while High Behind leaped and writhed.

Then the latigo popped and he went backward through the air, still clinging to the stallion's rope. He felt the scratch of thorny bushes, the impact of polished stones. He gripped the hackamore, and his light went out.

When Johnny Lightfoot came out of his trance, he was riding again, only now he was tied to the horn and the horse that he rode was not rough old High Behind but the golden stallion of his dreams. They were trotting up a cañon so deep and narrow that the walls cut out the light of the moon, but before him, leading the way, Johnny could see another horseman. Then he went out again.

When he woke up again, groaning, he lay face down across the saddle, lashed on like a deer, and on his lips there was the salt taste of blood. Ropes bit at his wrists and ankles, his back burned like fire, and his head seemed encased in an iron band, against which his pulse beat throbbed furiously. His brain reeled and he was conscious only of the gentle motion of his steed, an ambling trot that lulled him to sleep.

He woke again, long after, and he was lying in a cave from whose roof, like crystal pendants, long stalactites hung down with an eerie suggestion of splendor. In the pale light of dawn bats were fluttering past his couch, seeking their clinging places in the darkness beyond. Lightfoot sat up, laying one hand on his throbbing head, and at a stab of pain he clutched at his back. His shirt was wet with blood.

For an instant, seeing the eerie splendor of the crystals overhead and the bats flitting past, he wondered whether he was in heaven or hell. But at the feel of the fresh blood, it came back to him instantly—the fight over the horses, the sting of buckshot as he fled, then the ride up a dark, narrow cañon.

But who had brought him up here? And why had they left him, to welter uncared for in his blood? He listened intently as a distant noise came to his ears then. Clearly and distinctly he heard the *whang* of a heavy rifle and a staccato of answering shots. A battle was on, and at the memory of Val Bodie he rolled over and crept out of the cave.

A tangle of wild clematis hung down over its entrance, and, as he peered out, he saw the stallion over which they had fought, standing tied and still burdened with his saddle. There was a fence across the cañon, ancient willows lined the creek, and over the white stones a stream of water flowed, crystal clear, inviting him to drink. He rose weakly to his feet and staggered down to its brink, and, as he drank and washed his face, the stallion nickered appealingly, pulling back against his rope.

"Poor old horse," murmured Johnny, crawling over to the tree. With what seemed the last of his strength, he untied the tangled ropes and let him go down to the creek. Then he dropped back exhausted, for every effort he made started his wounds to bleeding afresh. The stallion sighed and sipped again, but at a noise from down the cañon he snorted and raised his head. Lightfoot heard the sound of approaching feet and wriggled feebly back toward the cave, but halfway across the open the last of his strength left him and he fell face down in the dirt.

Someone came and stood over him. He saw the tip of a buckskin moccasin and the butt of a gun on the ground. But as he raised his eyes, he beheld a woman's face, surrounded by a nimbus of golden hair. It was the moon maiden, flushed and hurried, and, even as she gazed, she turned and looked behind her.

"Who are you?" she asked in a low, anxious voice. "I found you last night and hid you in the cave. If my father finds you here, he will kill you."

"My name's Lightfoot," responded Johnny. "I saw you . . . down at Night Water. But somebody shot me in the back."

"That was Val Bodie," she said. "He tried to steal Paynim, and now he's coming up the cañon. Let me drag you into the cave, where nobody will find you. Because I can't bear to see you killed."

"Neither can I," grumbled Johnny Lightfoot grimly. "Can't you do something for my back?"

"Not now," she answered, taking hold of his hands and dragging him, willy-nilly, into the cave. "My father sent me back to get some more cartridges." And, dropping him inside the entrance, she deftly wiped out his tracks and sped away down the trail.

Lightfoot thrust out his head and stared after her curiously, as she darted into another and larger cave. Its door was only a cowhide, suspended by strips of rawhide.

When she came out, she bore an armful of cartridge boxes that she dropped into the pockets of her buckskin skirt. Then, snatching up her rifle, she ran off down the trail as swift and agile as a deer.

My Lord, he breathed to himself as the shooting burst out afresh, *she's a fighter, or I miss my guess. But how in the hell did she get up this cañon? And that horse I stole is tame.*

He glanced across the creek, where the golden stallion was peacefully feeding, and his eyes grew big as he watched. Here was the leader of the wild horses that he had chased at Night Water, and that Val Bodie had tried so long to trap, browsing placidly on willow shoots not ten feet away from him—with a saddle on his back. It was Lightfoot's own saddle, and the hackamore on its nose was the one he had put there himself. Yet down on the dry lakebed the stallion had fought like the devil.

"Here, Paynim," he called softly, using the name he had heard her use, and the horse pricked his ears and stared. But Paynim remembered the battles they had fought—he snorted and drew away. "A regular pet," muttered Johnny, looking him over enviously. Then, at a thought, he glanced up and down the cañon for some possible way of escape. But it was boxed in—there was no way out. He was trapped within these walls that rose thousands of feet high, and only the good will of this woman could save him, for he was wounded and unable to ride. Yet he was the man who had stolen Paynim, and Bodie had in turn taken the horse from him.

There was a *boom* from down the cañon, the loud-mouthed roar of a rifle, and a *crackling* of distant shots. Bodie had discovered at last the hidden pasture of the horses and he was trying to force his way in. If he succeeded, then Johnny Lightfoot could look for no mercy, for he had robbed Val Bodie of his prey. Next to whiskey Bodie loved women—but the golden horses of Toógahboth had long been the apple of his eye. At one stroke Lightfoot had deprived him of two prizes—the moon maiden and the stallion on which she rode.

Lightfoot listened anxiously as the shooting came nearer. Yet even if Bodie failed to force the narrow passageway, what hope had the future for him? The girl herself had told him that her father would kill him if he found him in this hidden retreat. He crawled back from the entrance to the shelter of some pack saddles, and crouched down to endure his pain; until at last, outlined against the light of the entrance, he saw a head bob up. It dodged back, and for a moment he felt the cold fear of death. Then it rose up again and his blurred eyes caught the vision of a nimbus of golden hair. The maiden had come back, but she was looking behind her down the cañon. He heard the sullen roar of guns.

She stood at gaze, like a sentinel guarding the secret of the cave. Then she stooped down suddenly and crept in toward him, and he felt her hot breath on his cheek. She leaned closer, feeling his face with small, clutching hands as if she feared to find him dead, and a quick tear splashed down between.

"He is coming!" she gasped. "You must stay here and hide." And she dropped a bundle of food and fled. But of this man who came Lightfoot knew nothing, except that his coming meant death.

Chapter Twelve

The noise of gunfire ceased abruptly, and Johnny Lightfoot lay listening for the sound of approaching footsteps—for the big, booming voice of his enemy, Val Bodie, or the voice of the moon maiden's father.

Whoever he was, he had inspired in his daughter a fear fully as great as that of the ruthless Bodie, who had promised to shoot Lightfoot on sight. But no footsteps came and Lightfoot became conscious of a hunger that gnawed at his vitals. Even while he listened for the coming of his enemies, he ate ravenously of the dried meat and bread.

They had had a battle at the entrance to the cañon, that same narrow gateway between frowning walls of schist that Lightfoot had watched through his glasses. It was not hard to guess who the Indian devil was who had terrorized the Indians for years. He was a white man, the owner of the band of golden horses that watered at Toógahboth. And when at last his stallion had been caught and the secret of his hiding place discovered, the old man had cast aside all pretense of being a devil and stepped into the open, shooting.

Hours of waiting dragged by and a fox peered into the cave, attracted by the smell of the meat. But when Lightfoot stirred, he scampered away, only to creep back, accompanied by his mate. They came closer, with that strange tameness that the wild stallion had shown, and Lightfoot remembered the silver foxes that had run at the horses' heads. The foxes, the horses, even the ghost maiden that rode them when the moon was at its full, all were mortal as himself—all dwelt in this hidden cañon. And the Indian devil of Enúpi Kai was the master of them all. Johnny threw out scraps of meat for the foxes to gnaw on and dozed off in a fevered sleep.

He was awakened by a hand laid upon his brow, and the moon maiden leaned over him, smiling. She had crept in unperceived and he caught the smell of arnica as he felt a wet cloth on his head.

"It is all right," she said soothingly. "The men have gone away and my father is guarding the gateway. Just let me bathe your head and put some medicine on your wounds . . . and, when you are well, you can go."

She washed the blood from the matted bruise, where he had fallen among the rocks, and Lightfoot lay quietly as with a pan of hot water she soaked off his dirt-encrusted shirt.

"Oh!" she exclaimed as in the half light of the cave she beheld his quivering back. "Did he do that . . . the man who caught me?"

"I reckon so." Lightfoot shuddered. "Feel around for those buckshot. Don't mind in the least if I kick a bit . . . dig 'em out."

"They went in and came out again," she said at last, after following the course of the pellets. "You must have been leaning over when he shot."

"Mighty lucky," he grumbled. "Poor old High Behind got most of it. Well, bandage me up good, so I can get out of here tonight. And put on lots of arnica."

"You'd better stay," she suggested as she worked over the wounds. "You'll die if you don't lie still. And if you go outside, those bad men will kill you. Stay here . . . I'll keep you hidden."

"What will your old man say if he finds me?" Johnny demanded.

She blushed and turned away.

"I . . . I'll hide you," she promised. "Although he says that all men are bad. He says the first man that gets in here and gets out again alive will come back and take everything we've got."

"Oho," spoke up Johnny. "So that's what's the matter with him. He's afraid of losing his horses."

"He says men are all bad, and we ought to keep away from them," she said with a fleeting smile. "But . . . but I've never seen any, so how can I tell? That is, until I saw you."

"Never seen any men?" repeated Johnny Lightfoot incredulously. "Been shut up in this cañon all your life?"

"I've seen them riding by," she admitted. "But he drives every man away."

"He must be crazy," he muttered. "But, say, I saw you once . . . down on the lakebed."

"He doesn't know it," she confessed, "but I go down there at night. When the moon shines, it seems as if these big walls would smother me. I've just got to get out and see the great world. And we turn out the horses then. At first there were only four of them, but now we have eleven and there isn't enough grass up the cañon. So every full moon Father opens the lower gate and lets them go down on the plain. Isn't it beautiful down there, at night?"

"It's like a dream," he answered. "The first time

I saw you, I thought you had come down from the moon."

"Oh, did you?" she cried, laughing rapturously. "Did you see me down there . . . riding? I get so lonely I just can't stand it. But what were you doing at Night Water?"

"I'd heard about the horses, and how beautiful they were," he evaded. "So I went there and hid . . . to watch them."

"If Father had seen you . . . ," she began, then stopped and bit her lip. "He kills people," she said at last.

"So I've heard." He nodded. "But what does he do it for? I thought the horses were wild."

"Oh, he's . . . strange," she replied, bandaging his wounds up nervously. "He's afraid they'll steal his mine."

"Mine?" he echoed, startled.

"He's got one . . . somewhere," she stated. But Johnny knew there was only one *somewhere* where the mine was likely to be hidden, and that was right up that cañon. But she had already told him too much and he did not pursue the subject.

"Oh, that's nothing." He laughed. "All these old prospectors are that way. And they think it's worth millions and millions."

"Yes . . . he does," she admitted naïvely. "All he thinks about is gold. He talks to himself, and threatens to kill people if they follow him back to his mine."

"You look out," Johnny warned, "that he doesn't kill you. I believe your old man is crazy."

"He acts very strange," she said. "And Mother, before she died, told me to run away somewhere. But there isn't any place I can go. I never believed before that men were so cruel . . . he claims they're just like beasts. But when Val Bodie caught me . . . down at the lake last night. . . ."

She bowed her head, to wink back the tears, and Johnny struggled up from where he lay.

"Now, here," he began, "don't you worry about him. I'll take care of you. What's your name?"

"Diana," she sobbed, "Diana Morgan. But if Father finds you here, I know he will kill you. And maybe he'll kill me, too."

She dropped her head against his breast and continued weeping. Johnny held her helplessly. Here was a woman so innocent she was no more than a child, and yet, as he felt her body against his, he experienced a strange sort of fear. She was a woman too innocent for the great world outside. He was afraid, and yet he thrilled at her touch.

"Never mind now," he soothed. "I'll try and come back for you if I ever get out of here alive. And if you'll give me a gun, I'll protect you against your father, in case he tries to kill you. But you'd better go away, before he comes back and finds us. And, besides, you don't know who I am."

"Yes, I do," she answered, looking up with a smile as she brushed away a tear. "I was watching when you crawled out and untied Paynim, so he could go to the creek and drink."

"I like horses," admitted Johnny, "and that's why I did it. But your old man was right, and don't forget it . . . most men are a mighty rough lot."

"But didn't you ride in, when Val Bodie caught me, and make him let me go? Oh, I'll never forget how terrible it was, when he grabbed me . . . and began to laugh."

She shuddered, and Johnny let her lie where she

was until her fit of weeping had passed. He even stroked her hair and told her not to cry. And then he tried again.

"Now, listen," he began, "and I'll tell you how that happened . . . and the kind of *hombre* I am. I didn't come down there to save you. I'm a horse ketcher, savvy? And I came there to ketch that horse. I seen him tied to the stake and I was just sneaking up when you rode in on that beautiful mare . . . and, of course, I had to hide. But when Bodie jumped out and grabbed you, I'll have to admit I was mad. So I rode in on him, shooting, and gave you back your horse, while I cut loose the hobbles on Paynim. That's what I was there for . . . to get away with him. If Bodie hadn't run out and filled me full of buckshot, you'd never have seen your Paynim horse again."

"What? Were you trying to steal Paynim?" she demanded indignantly, suddenly bounding up to her feet. "Why, when I found you wounded, Paynim was standing right over you. He knew you had saved him, and he wouldn't stir a step until I put you up on his back."

"He's a wonderful horse"—Johnny sighed—"the most beautiful horse I've seen. That's why I wanted to steal him."

"Steal Paynim!" she cried. "Don't you know what would have happened to you? My father would have followed you and killed you, then and there. That's his way of dealing with horse thieves."

"I reckon so," responded Johnny, stretching out on the bed to ease his aching back. "But say, Diana . . . don't you think you'd better go? Because if your old man finds me, who'll come back and take care of you, when you try to leave this hole?"

"Well, it won't be any horse thief!" she flared back angrily. "Because that's one thing that Father just hates. When Paynim was stolen, he rode clear to Mormon Lake on purpose to kill Val Bodie. But while he was gone, Bodie's men came back, and I saw Paynim tied to that stake. If I had just waited a little longer, Father would have killed them all. And so you're a horse thief, too?"

"Well, you might call it that, if you were mad enough," said Johnny. "I thought the horses were wild."

"What . . . those horses?" She laughed. "Can't you tell a real thoroughbred? Why, Selim, Paynim's father, was the best horse in Kentucky, when my father brought him West. They're racehorses. Of course they're not wild."

"They didn't have any brands," defended Lightfoot. "How the hell could I tell they were yours? Nobody knowed that you lived here . . . and they don't know yet. Go on, now, and leave me alone."

She drew away from him hatefully, as if at her feet a rattlesnake had given his warning. Then she turned and started away, but at the mouth of the cave she came back.

"Here's some water," she said, throwing down a canteen. "And I'll bring you some grub, by and by. But I'll give you to understand I'm a Morgan from Kentucky, and no man can sass me like that."

"All right, then," mumbled Johnny Lightfoot. But when she was gone, he sat up and felt his bruised head. He had lost the power to think, to extricate himself from difficulties, and now he had offended the only person in the world who could get him out of that cañon alive. She was lonely, like a child shut up in a closet or a man lost on some desert island. He should have treated her gently, instead of sending her away and bragging about stealing her horse. But the gold mine, the thoroughbreds, the Morgans of Kentucky. He felt his head again and muttered to himself. Perhaps he had bumped it a little too hard.

Chapter Thirteen

Johnny Lightfoot fell asleep with a feeling of guilt, of misfortune, and of worse to come. He woke up sweating, a roaring voice in his ears—a man cursing as few men can curse. Crouching low, he peered out, expecting to see him at the cave mouth, but the voice came from farther away.

"Damn them all!" it thundered. "They are trying to steal my mine. They are trying to get my horses and my daughter. They are nothing but scoundrels and cut-throats. But I killed one ... I saw him fall ... and the rest slunk away ... Val Bodie and his scurvy crew! By the gods, how I would love to stand them in a row and kill them, a man at a time!"

In the bright light outside, Lightfoot could see the man pace by, a rifle in his hand, only his buckskin leggings showing as he strode up the trail to the fence.

"Hey, Selim!" he called with senile joviality. "Hey, Turco! Hey, Regulus! How are you? Did those rascal half-breeds try to trap you at the water hole? And here's my noble Paynim, as I live. Diana, how did Paynim get back? Come up here! Can't you hear me talking?"

Johnny saw her moccasins as she hurried past, and then in a low voice she began to tell her story.

"What's that?" he bellowed. "You say Bodie had him caught and staked out in front of his trap?

Now tell me the truth. Who helped you get him back? I know you couldn't do it by yourself."

"I don't know who he was," she answered meekly. "But a man on a high-backed horse who had been hiding among the trees rode out and cut the hobbles. He threw me Moonbeam's rope and told me to ride."

"Moonbeam!" he broke in. "Did they have her tied up, too?"

"Well, no," she faltered. "I rode down to get Paynim, and the horse hunters dashed out and caught her. They caught me, too, but this man charged in shooting and drove the whole band away. And then he gave me the ropes and told me to ride . . . and just as I looked back, Bodie shot him."

"Poor fellow," pronounced her father. "Some member of the band in whom a spark of chivalry still lived. And so Bodie murdered him. But what was that about his horse? You say he was very high behind?"

"Yes, and straddled when he loped. I didn't see him distinctly."

"Hah! I know the rascal well!" exclaimed her father triumphantly. "He's a wolf in sheep's clothing if he pretended to turn Paynim loose. I saw him at Mormon Lake, where he raced Bodie's Fly and asked me to hold the stakes. He's a horse hunter himself and he came in on purpose to catch our horses and sell them. He was traveling with an Injun, a cursed Shoshone that was always trying to track me to my mine . . . until I laid for him one day and put a bullet through his neck. You say Val Bodie killed him?"

"They were fighting," she evaded, "and I saw his

horse run past. But don't you think he was a very kind man?"

"He's a rascal, I tell you!" the old man thundered. "Every man in this country is a scoundrel and an outlaw. They've all fled here to escape punishment for their crimes. There isn't an honest man in all this broad country . . . they're all criminals and fugitives from justice, ready to prey on anyone they meet. And as for this gay young blade who saved you so handsomely, he's a mustanger by profession and enjoys the cognomen of Horse-Ketchum, bestowed by his Injun friend!"

"Why, I think," she defended, "that's a very pretty name. And I wished I could have thanked him for saving my life. He saved Paynim and Moonbeam, too."

"Yes, he saved them!" mocked her father. "But if Bodie had let him live, you'd have seen this same Horse-Ketchum riding off across the valley with both of them. I know him, for I heard him defy Bodie himself when he warned him out of the country. He had a specimen of the rock that Breyfogle found . . . the identical ore of my mine. Washed out, I suppose, by some terrific cloudburst and picked up as the Dutchman wandered past. But now that my hiding place has been discovered by these rascals, I'll play the last card I've got. I'm going back to drill some more holes under that gateway and blow the whole wall down."

"Oh, and shut us all in?" she cried. "Then how will we ever get out?"

"That is something," he said, "that gives me no concern whatever. Val Bodie has found me and he'll never give up till he forces his way up this cañon. But I'll show the scoundrelly rogue that a Morgan cannot be intimidated. I'm a fighter."

"But, Father," she pleaded, "we'll run out of food. And, besides, I don't want to be shut in."

Her voice rose with tragic intensity, but he answered her impatiently, and Lightfoot heard him striding past. By now he knew who this devil man was—he was Frying-Pan George, the prospector. He it was who had shot Captain Jack in the neck. He had been at Mormon Lake when the horse race had been run, and held the stakes—and the ore. What chance, then, for Johnny if the half-crazed old prospector found him hiding inside his cañon?

Lightfoot lay listening to the sound of drills and hammers *clinking* together, while above the *clatter* of steel he could hear Diana's father giving orders as he bestowed his load. Hammers and drills, and a canteen of water, and a spoon to clean out the holes, until at last down the cañon the voices receded and Johnny crept out.

If he stayed inside the gateway until the fatal shots were fired, he would be caged up in that cañon with a madman—and Frying-Pan George would shoot. Yet how could he escape, how find a way out with the old man guarding the entrance?

Dusk was gathering in the deep valley, but high up on the eastern walls he could see the glow of the sun. In a hole like that, walled in by towering cliffs, there was no way out but one. Slowly and painfully he started down the path toward the entrance, but his strength was too far spent and he crept back to the crystal cave.

Evening came and the bats one by one fluttered past him on their way to hunt for gnats. They alone could escape from this abyss among the peaks. But if Johnny Lightfoot gained the open, he would be no better off, for the night riders would be watching the gateway. They had located the hiding place of Frying-Pan George, the source of his mysterious ore, and the specimen of gold rock they had taken from him would add new fuel to their greed.

It was Breyfogle ore, and they knew for themselves now that Frying-Pan's ore was the same. What to them were the golden horses they had come to catch? The greatest treasure of Death Valley had been suddenly revealed to them and they would watch the cañon night and day.

Lightfoot stretched out wearily behind his barricade of pack saddles, well content with the poor comfort of a canteen of water and a sack of jerked meat and bread. He was safe within his cave, with Diana to care for him. When his strength came back, he could ride.

He was roused up at dawn by the resonant voice of Morgan, returning to the cave below. Then the smell of smoke came to him and the incense of roasting coffee, but Diana did not appear. Hours passed, and he gnawed hungrily at the sticks of fried meat, and, when the foxes appeared at the mouth of the cave, he did not respond to their wiles. First one and then the other would creep a little closer, crouching down expectantly, wagging their bushy tails like dogs, yapping and chattering as they sniffed the meat.

"Here," he said at last, holding out a sliver of jerky. After watching him in silence, the bolder of the two reached out and snatched it away. They were tame, as tame as dogs, and, although his food was running low, Lightfoot tolled them on with more and more. It served to wile away the time and lighten the tedium of his confinement—to break in on his anxious thoughts. The foxes were sitting before him, their black-tipped noses out, when a head appeared in the doorway. Then swiftly Diana came gliding into the cave, and Johnny could see she was pleased.

In the dim light of the cave her eyes beamed on him approvingly as she passed him a pannikin of food, but she touched her lips for silence. Then she sat down, watching him as he poured out the hot coffee—meanwhile holding the pet foxes in her lap. But at a sound outside the entrance she leaped up like a flash, and Lightfoot was left alone.

Evening came and the fretful voice of the old man rose up as he called for his powder and tools. Perhaps that very night he would make good his threat and blast down the walls of the gateway. Lightfoot listened anxiously as their voices died away, and then, despite his stiffness, he crawled out of his cave and slipped away up the trail.

A strong fence, with a stile, blocked the cañon from wall to wall, and beyond it, along the creekbed, there was an irrigated garden with corn and beans and cabbages in orderly rows. Then the cañon opened out into a broad valley among the peaks—a valley dotted with mesquite trees among which he could see the horses, reaching up to browse on the tips. Feed was short already, and not for many a moon would they graze on the salt meadows of Toógahboth.

Lightfoot climbed over the stile and sat down inside the fence to look out the rimrock for a pass. It rose sheerly to the south, and the waning light of day showed frowning ramparts of black to the east.

But the north wall of the valley was more broken, with streaks of white, and a trail ran along its base. He hobbled up it, bent over like an old man with the ache of his wounded back, and around the first point he came suddenly on a cañon that split the wall in twain.

There was a path, deeply worn, winding up among the boulders and over broken ledges of quartz, and on the farther hillside, like a gopher mound, a dump of rock had been thrown out. Lightfoot quickened his pace. In such a place as this, with white quartz and limestone and a por-phyry contact on the east—in such a place gold might be found. The dump showed that mining had been done. A sudden thrill went over him as, trampled in the dust, he saw the greasy wrapper of a powder stick. Then at a turn of the trail he beheld a black tunnel with a big dump of waste at its mouth.

His knees, which had been so weak, suddenly regained their strength. He ran forward and stared into the hole, which smelled of dead powder fumes and sweat. In a pile by the entrance there was a heap of picked ore, and he knelt down, trembling, to examine it.

It's gold! he cried silently, snatching up a chunk of rock. *By the gods, it's Frying-Pan's mine!*

Chapter Fourteen

With a piece of gold quartz still clutched in his hand, and panting and groaning with the weight of his pain, Lightfoot hurried back to the mouth of his cave, stooping low like a man that hides. He had found the mine that Frying-Pan George had kept hidden for twenty years—the lost Breyfogle Mine!

But what good was it to him, who sought only a way to escape? Yet he clung to the ore, with its pinpoints of gold, and, as he sank down, he held it to his eyes. Yes, imbedded in its matrix of blackened quartz, the mother of all evil gazed out at him with a pure and steady glow. It was the Breyfogle ore that for twenty years desert prospectors had sought and died in the attempt. His heart leaped as he realized what wealth lay hidden here in this cañon with the one, guarded gate. And he had thought Diana's father crazy. But to hold a mine like that many a man would live as he had, shut away from all the world.

Lightfoot sat dreaming, oblivious of the shadows that the moon cast among the trees until, before his eyes, a shadow rose up and the moon maiden stood before him. The buckskin suit was gone and in its place she wore a dress, long and sweeping and gracefully draped.

"Were you waiting for me?" she asked as he sat staring in astonishment.

Johnny forgot his dreams. Her voice was so eager, her manner so sweet, her desire to please so apparent. "Sure was," he answered gallantly. "But, I declare, I hardly knew you. You're just like a lady out of a book."

"Like Maid Marion or Rebecca, or the Lady of Shalot?" she mocked. "I've read about them, over and over. But they all lived so long ago. What is the world like now? Do the women wear dresses like these?"

"Nope, not nearly so handsome." he responded admiringly. "You sure look fine, now . . . Diana."

"Oh, thank you," she replied with a curtsy. "This is one my mother made. She used to send out when Father went for supplies and order the most beautiful things. But now that she's gone all he brings me is calico . . . the kind they sell to squaws."

"Well, sit down," he invited, "if it won't get your dress dirty. And say, Diana, what's he doing down there? Is he going to shoot those rocks down tonight?"

"Oh, no," she answered lightly, "not for two or three nights. Perhaps he won't do it at all. There's something about the full moon that seems to make him worse. But now that he's slept, he's better."

"You mean he don't cuss and barrel around the way he did? No fooling, he had me scared. Are you dead sure he won't come up here and find us together, and fill me full of holes?"

"I'm not sure of anything." She sighed, gathering her skirt up and sinking to the ground. "But I thought, while you were here, I'd like to put this dress on and pretend to be a lady again. My mother was a Chatfield, one of the oldest Kentucky families, and every day, while Father was working in his mine, she'd instruct me in the ways of society. When I was sixteen years old, she made me this silk dress . . . for my coming-out party, or debut. But I've had it four years, and you're the first young man that I've had the pleasure to meet."

"The pleasure is all mine," responded Johnny Lightfoot politely. "And if it wasn't for that charge of buckshot in my back, I'd rise up and make my bow."

"Oh, dear!" she cried. "And I haven't looked at it all day! Did you keep the cloth wet with arnica?"

"Yes, and kept right still," he answered. "I reckon it'll soon be well."

"I'm sorry," she began hastily, "that I spoke the way I did . . . about horse thieves and all the rest. But I'm a Morgan, I reckon, and Mother used to say they were all a hot-tempered lot."

"That's all right," mumbled Lightfoot. "Mighty glad you came back. I was afraid I'd lost you for good."

"Well, I was huffed," she confessed, "but when I looked in and saw you feeding my foxes, I knew we just hadn't understood. I'm hot-headed, and so are you. But I'm not angry now. Will you shake hands? And let's be friends."

"Suits me," replied Johnny, reaching out the grimy paw. "And I'm sorry for what I said. But I was so badly scared your old man would bust in on us, and maybe have a killing, right there, that I didn't care what I said."

"I knew it." She nodded. "Afterward. And I knew you were not a horse thief. You just thought our horses were wild."

"Sure," Johnny assented. "There wasn't a mark on 'em. And the law is . . . any horse that's running without a brand belongs to the first man that ropes him. But that Paynim horse." He sighed. "I took a big chance . . . and I'd take a big chance again."

"How big?" she asked, after a meditative silence.

Johnny saw her breast heave expectantly. "A big one," he repeated. "But don't you worry, Diana. I won't ride off on him, when I go."

"Oh, of course not," she murmured. "I didn't mean that. But why don't you stay here, Johnny?"

"What, and have your father find me, hiding out in this cave, and shoot me like a holed-up coyote? That's just what he'll do, and I know it."

"Oh, no," she protested feebly. "But . . . well, maybe you're right. Only, Johnny, couldn't you take me . . . when you go?"

A hush fell as he met her gaze in the moonlight— her eyes were as innocent as a child's. But she was a woman, a woman grown—and the world would not understand.

"If you could," she pleaded as he hesitated, "if you would . . . before he shuts us in. Then you could ride Paynim, and I would ride Moonbeam. And Paynim would always be yours. I would talk to him and tell him that you were his new master, and he'd follow you like a dog. Oh, couldn't you take me, Johnny? I'm afraid here . . . all alone."

"No," he decided. "Your old man would kill me. If it wasn't for him, now . . . well, maybe I'll come back . . . but I can't take you with me, Diana."

"But why?" she asked after a silence.

Lightfoot took her hand. "Diana." he said, "I'd sure like to do it. With you and old Paynim . . . and Moonbeam, too. But, no, it can't be done. You don't know the people outside. People like Hank, and

Val Bodie. Didn't your mother ever tell you always to think what people might say, and not take a chance with strangers?"

"Why, no," she answered wonderingly. "She told me always to be good, and to do only what was right. But there weren't any people, you know."

"Well, I'll have to tell you, then," replied Johnny bluntly, "that people are a mighty tough lot. And they always think the worst. Where the devil would I take you if we got away alive? Have you got any folks in these parts?"

"My folks are in Kentucky," she responded. "But my father is hiding from them all. I don't know why it is, but the Chatfields and the Tollivers have fought each other for years. It was a feud, and my father was compelled to kill a man. So he came out here to hide."

"You bet," agreed Lightfoot. "I understand all that. Those Kentucky mountaineers are always fighting each other. And I've heard about the Chatfields, too."

"He killed six of them," she went on steadily, "and then he started West. It was Mother that persuaded him to go. Her family were Chatfields, but she just couldn't stand it, to see her husband drawn into it. So he sold out his business and everything he had and they joined an emigrant train West. But his horses he wouldn't sell . . . they were just like children to him . . . and he took the four thoroughbreds along. Old Selim is living still."

"Sure enough?" said Johnny. "Are they genuine Kentucky thoroughbreds? But how did you folks get here?"

"I don't know," she answered pensively. "Father and Mother refused to talk about it. But one time he showed me from the top of the high cliff the spot where the emigrants all died. It is over at the base of that big, black mountain . . . and his folks, of course, believe him dead. But he escaped to this cañon, after a fight with the Indians. And when he found his mine, Mother was willing to stay here, because the Tollivers would never quit looking for him. But before she died, she told me Father was queer and it was better perhaps to go."

"Yes, but where to?" asked the practical Johnny Lightfoot. "I'm game to take you out, if you've got any folks to. . . ."

"Listen, Johnny," she appealed, moving closer and gazing up at him, "I haven't got a kinswoman in the world. But I can ride as well as you can . . . I've ridden all my life . . . and I'm not afraid any more. When I saw you first, you looked so terrible, all covered with blood and dirt. But Paynim stood right over you and I knew you had been kind to him . . . that's why I brought you here. And then Christopher and Columbus, my dear little foxes, went right up and fed out of your hand. So I know you're a good man and I'm willing to go anywhere, if you'll only take me away."

She laid her head on his shoulder and leaned against him expectantly, and Lightfoot put out his arm. She was a child, he told himself, and held her close as he pondered an answer, but she turned and kissed him quickly on the cheek.

"I knew you'd hold me." She sighed. "No one does it any more, since Mother passed away. You can kiss me, too, if you wish."

She raised her lips impulsively, but Johnny dodged away. "Hold on, now." He laughed. "Isn't this getting pretty familiar, considering our short acquaintance? How old are you, anyway, Diana?"

"I'm old enough," she answered, "to have my own way. Are you going to take me with you when you go?"

"Why, sure," responded Johnny lightly. "But what's that got to do with kissing?"

"It's got everything," she declared. And before he could resist, she had drawn him into a clinging embrace. "I just love you," she breathed, and, as her lips met his, Johnny forgot duty and danger and everything.

"That's good," he said, and kissed her again, before he pushed her reluctantly away. The glamorous moonlight had played him a trick—or perhaps it was Diana's kiss—for now he thought no longer of gold and a swift escape. He was content, like the lotus-eaters, to dream.

Chapter Fifteen

On his couch within the cave Johnny Lightfoot tossed and groaned, for his wounds pained the more as they healed. But while he lay in the black silence, he remembered, like a fantasy, Diana sitting in the moonlight, Diana in clinging silk, with the moonshine in her hair and innocence in her eyes, Diana like a child, creeping into his arms— Diana demanding to be kissed. He turned on his bed and moaned. Then sleep came, and he awoke to a shadow hovering over him, and outside the cave it was day.

In the gloom of the cave he saw her, smiling anxiously, moving softly as she set down her tray. But as she stooped down, he closed his eyes. He was weak, and he had forgotten the stern words he wished to say, to protect her from herself. Perhaps she would go away. He stirred, and swiftly across his brow he felt the touch of her hair. Then her cool cheek pressed his, there was the ghost of a kiss, and she laughed as he opened his eyes.

"It is late," she whispered, "and Father is asleep. Those terrible men have gone."

"They'll be back," he grumbled. "I know that Bodie gang. They'll get up this cañon yet."

"No, they won't," she retorted, beginning to wash his grimy hands. "My father has expected this to happen for years, and he's got his plans all made. At the foot of the waterfall, where we climbed up that night, he has drilled deep holes in the bedrock. One blast will blow it out and leave a solid wall of stone, twenty or thirty feet high at the least."

"They'll fill it up with rocks," predicted Lightfoot, "or put up a ladder some night."

"Yes, and then," she cried triumphantly, "he'll set off his big blast and blow the south wall down on top of them. It's hundreds of feet high and split from top to bottom. Only think, if it ever came down."

"My Lord!" exclaimed Lightfoot. "Has he loaded his holes yet? Say, Diana . . . just look at my back."

"No, only the bottom ones," she soothed. "Oh, dear . . . you've hurt it again."

"Never mind," answered Lightfoot. "There's one thing dead certain. I'm going to get out of this cañon before he touches off the blasts."

"Then you must lie still, and be quiet," she admonished, "and not go off, the way you did last night. I found your tracks up the cañon, where you went to the mine. Big boot tracks. But I wiped them out."

"Yes . . . looking for some trail to get out of here," he explained.

Diana glanced at him shrewdly. "If Father sees one track around his mine . . . ," she began.

"I know." Johnny nodded. "He'll kill me."

"He'll think you're trying to steal his gold," she ended anxiously. "And, oh, dear, I'm so afraid. But I've got it all planned, and here's some gold we can take with us. I picked it up down in the creek."

She passed over a buckskin sack, and Johnny forgot his qualms as he felt the weight of the gold.

"Lord," he breathed. "Can you pick it up like that?"

"Here's a piece I brought for you." she answered, and dropped a big nugget into his hand. Then she smiled and rattled on, while he listened in stunned silence, absently hefting the weight of the gold. "I was so excited last night, I couldn't sleep a wink, but Father didn't come home. I hate to run off and leave him . . . and who'd feed my dear foxes? Poor Christopher and Columbus, I love them so much. And all the horses, too. We used to have such fun down on the lakebed at night. They all know their names . . . I raised them from colts. But there was nobody here to talk to. Poor Father . . . all he thinks of is his mine."

"Is it rich?" asked Lightfoot guardedly. "And, say, what does he do with the ore?"

"Oh, he pounds it out in those Indian potholes, where they used to grind up mesquite beans. And then he washes it out in the creekbed and puts it in buckskin sacks. It's beautiful up here in the spring-time, when the pussy willows and mesquite trees are in flower. Could you stand it to live here, Johnny?"

"Not me," Lightfoot declared. "This cañon is too small. I like to ramble around, ketching horses and prospecting, and entering matching races."

"But, oh, think," she exclaimed, "how Paynim can run! He can beat any horse in the world. When Father let them out, to feed down below, I used to run away every night. When he was asleep, I'd take Moonbeam and ride after them. With Christopher and Columbus, too. And we'd play on the lake un-til the foxes were tired out . . . and then we'd all race home. But now that Val Bodie has found where we live . . . do you think he's out there, Johnny?"

"You bet your life," asserted Lightfoot. "And that's one thing I'm afraid of. If I take you out with me, like I promised last night. . . ."

"Oh, but, Johnny," she cried, clutching his hand, "you must take me! Think of being shut in here . . . with him!"

"Yes, and think of being caught by that big, fat Val Bodie . . . and me, maybe, too weak to ride."

"But I'd be on Moonbeam," she protested. "And nobody could catch me . . . on her."

"They caught you once," he returned. "And say, where're my guns? Did you find them, down where I fell?"

"I saw them," she confessed, "a pistol and a rifle. But you were so heavy, Johnny . . . after I'd lifted you up, I just rode away without them."

"I see." He nodded, and lay in deep thought as she drenched his back with arnica. The danger from his wounds was past, but they stiffened him and impeded his movements. After a short ride he would weaken, especially if it came to a chase. Yet any night now a fresh battle might spring up, or the mouth of the narrow cañon might be closed. There was danger in delay—but even more in flight.

"Diana," he said at last, "I've got to have a rifle. And a couple of six-shooters, too. Can't you get them from your father?"

"Yes, I could," she said. "But he takes them all with him. And the minute he missed one. . . ."

"Well, just before I go, then," he assented. "I'll slip off while he's asleep."

"What? And not take me?" she gasped.

"I'll take you," he answered, "if you hold me to my promise . . . though how I ever came to make it is sure a mystery to me. You'd be lots safer here, Diana . . . and I swear I'll come back for you. . . ."

"Yes, but when you took his guns . . . and maybe Paynim, too. . . ."

"That's right," admitted Lightfoot. "Well, I'll wait a while, Diana. And when I do go. . . ."

"You'll take me." She smiled. And before Johnny knew it, she had kissed him and danced away.

Chapter Sixteen

There was something disconcerting, and even a trifle suspicious, about the way Diana put promises in Johnny's mouth and then stopped his lips with kisses. They were childish kisses, of course, but at the second occurrence Lightfoot began to have his doubts. All her life, so she said, she had lived within the portals of that gateway of solid stone. And yet, somewhere, in some way, she had learned to coax and wheedle and turn men from their purpose.

Better by far for both of them, with Val Bodie lingering near, if Lightfoot should slip out alone. Either afoot or on horseback he could travel and fight better—but Diana had had her way. And perhaps, he mused, her way would prove best.

Every day brought back his strength, and from the cliff above she could watch for Bodie and his gang. Johnny settled down comfortably, clean and fed and with newly bound wounds, and the memory of her soft hands seemed to soothe him to sleep.

When he awoke, that particular day had passed, and Morgan was shouting below.

"Where have you been?" he demanded imperiously. In the hush of evening Lightfoot could hear Diana answer him.

"I've been up on the cliff," she called, "and Val Bodie is coming back! There are twenty-two men and eight packs, and they're riding up the valley toward Night Water."

"Well, come down here," yelled her father, "and put me up some grub! Those rascals are determined to force their way up this cañon. But I'll show them, the cowardly whelps. I'll camp at the portals and give them a warm welcome if they come within range of my rifle. They think they can intimidate me, or creep in at night and murder me in my sleep. There's no doubt in my mind . . . they've come to kill us both in order to get possession of my mine."

His deep roar was muffled as he passed into his cave to get together his outfit and guns. When he came out, still cursing, Diana was doing pack duty, and they passed out of hearing down the cañon.

Johnny Lightfoot rose up and crept out of his cave—he felt caged, like a rat in a trap. Sooner or later, if he stayed here, the old man would find his hiding place, and then, without a gun, Johnny would be at his mercy. It was a sorry death to die.

The last rays of the dying sun painted the funereal cliffs blood red and an owl awoke echoes with his call. Night birds dipped down near him in the gloom of the cañon and the bats flitted noiselessly past. It was a grim, spooky spot.

Along the pasture fence the golden horses stood nickering, their heads in an eager row. They had come to the stile when they heard their master's voice, but in the hurry their begging had been forgotten.

Johnny watched as bold Paynim thrust his head beyond the rest, and then he hobbled toward him. His back was healing now, but at each forward stride the stiffened muscles seemed to creak. Yet here was the horse that had saved his life and he took him his last piece of bread. Paynim reached for it delicately, with his lips and not his teeth, and, as Johnny bestowed his peace offering, the horse suffered him to stroke his nose.

"By the gods," Lightfoot said in a low voice, "you're the top horse of the world, Paynim. And a thoroughbred, eh, from Kentucky? You wait till my back is well and we'll ride out of this hell hole."

Paynim shook his head and turned away. Not for one crust of bread and a pat on the nose would he let this strange horseman buy his friendship. He remembered the bite of a rope as it settled about his neck, the smashing fall, and the smothering hackamore. Then the long, stubborn fight as he was led away from his mates and his last, frenzied battle for freedom. But back at the water hole, ruthlessly tied to a stake and left to swelter in the heat, he had seen this same enemy ride in and cut him loose and lead him back toward his cañon. It was for that—and the drink of water when he stood tied near the creek—that Paynim had amended his views. But he was a thoroughbred, and not easily won.

The two foxes trotted up as Johnny sat on the stile, wagging their tails but sniffing at him dubiously. Then, down the trail, he saw Diana coming back—and the horses all crowded to the bars.

"No, Moonbeam," she said as she saw their eager heads, "we can never go back to Night Water. No, Paynim . . . no, Turco. Those bad men have come back." And she reached up to pat Paynim's neck. "They have come to stay this time," she went on, turning to Johnny. "Val Bodie and all his men."

"We're bottled up, then," he said, shrugging. "Isn't there any way out? Can't we find some trail up that cliff?"

"Only a mountain sheep can scale it," she responded. "And sometimes they slip and fall. When they come down to the spring, Father shoots them for jerked meat, and I know every path they use. We're shut in, Johnny . . . are you angry?"

She sat down beside him and took one of his hands in hers while she leaned her yellow-haired head against his. It was a way she had, and not for the world would Johnny have it otherwise.

"I'm not angry unless you are," he answered gallantly. "We've got lots of company, anyway."

"Who do you mean?" she asked.

"Why, I've got you . . . and you've got me," he said.

Diana tried to kiss him. "Isn't it wonderful," she breathed. "I'm so happy it just hurts. If you'd been a bad man, I don't know what I'd've done. You're the very first one . . . and I love you."

"That's good . . . that's capital," he praised, "only don't try to make me a pet. I'm kind of wild, you know, like an antelope. And if you pet 'em too much, they die."

"Yes, I know it," she answered gravely. "Or at least little mountain sheep do. But what do you really mean, Johnny? Don't you like to have me kiss you?"

"Oh, yes," he answered bluffly. "But you see it's this way, Diana . . . I never had a girl. And so I ain't used to being kissed."

"Well, neither am I . . . any more." She sighed. "But mother used to kiss me all the time."

"Poor little girl," he said.

She cuddled down into his arms, while the foxes crept close to her side. The moon, past its full, cast a pale glow on the cañon walls and the horses shuffled dejectedly away. Even the foxes fell to playing, but Diana did not stir.

"It's so long," she said at last, "since anybody cared for me. Have you got a mother, Johnny?"

"I've got nothing," returned Lightfoot, "except the horse I ride. And now I haven't even got a horse."

"Yes, you have," she asserted. "You've got Paynim, if you want him. Let's get your saddle and let him become used to it. I always ride them bareback, you know."

"I can ride 'em that way, too," replied Lightfoot. "But I'd sure like to mount him . . . just once. You don't reckon your old man will be back?"

"No, he's watching the gateway," she answered, skipping away. And she returned with the saddle on her arm. "Here, Paynim!" she called as she lowered the top bars and swung up over the rest. "They're jumpers," she explained, as she sat waiting in the moonlight. "We had to make the bars ten high. Oh, here he comes. Here, Paynim! And here's my Moonbeam, too. No, you can't go out the gate!"

She pushed their heads away as they leaned over the peeled poles and slipped a hair *mecate* on Paynim.

"Now, here's your horse, Johnny," she said, leading him over. "And Paynim, here's your master! Understand?"

She patted him on the neck as he snorted and drew back.

"No, Paynim," she commanded. "Now you stand! And, Johnny, you put on your saddle."

Slowly and quietly, while his heart beat hard, Johnny Lightfoot fastened the cinch. Then, at a word from Diana, he swung up into the saddle and took the end of the rope.

"Here, Moonbeam!" she summoned.

When the mare came trotting up, she mounted with a light, graceful leap. The two horses started off at a swift, rhythmic trot—they cantered, they galloped, they stopped. Even though his back was wounded, Johnny hardly felt a pang. It was the poetry of motion—it was speed. They turned and rode back, down the broad, level trail that the horses had worn to the gate, and then, in full flight, Diana swung over behind him and leaped back as Moonbeam swept past.

"Isn't it wonderful!" she exclaimed as they reined in at the gate, and Johnny patted his horse. His horse—the noble Paynim, whose sires for thousands of years had ranged the desert sands of Arabia! He stepped off and dropped the rope, and Paynim stood like a statue, head high, his sensitive ears intent.

"He hears something . . . ," began Johnny, and then, around his neck, he felt Diana's soft, clinging arms.

"He's waiting," she said.

At the touch of her form, Lightfoot felt a strange, wild thrill. She was panting from her exertion, her breath was warm on his cheek, and she drew his head slowly down. Then as she raised her upturned lips, he crushed them with kisses, holding her close, like a fluttering, ecstatic bird.

"Oh, Johnny!" she gasped. "It's been so lonely without you . . . without anybody that I could love. Do you mind?" And she kissed him again.

A madness came over him—his brain reeled, his heart beat harder. But as he held her, trembling, Paynim snorted and stepped back, and Lightfoot raised his eyes.

Across the top of the stile a long gun was moving toward him, its muzzle pointing straight at his head. And behind it, his face contorted, stood Frying-Pan George. Johnny ducked—and the gun went off. Then he ran, stunned and deafened by the thunder of the rifle, ran and dodged, and the gun roared again. But Diana had leaped forward and struck the barrel up, and he heard her voice calling: "Run!"

Johnny Lightfoot glanced back and saw them grappling for the rifle. Then, as he fled, he came on Paynim, dragging his *mecate* as he made off, and with one bound he pounced on the rope.

"Whoa, Paynim," he soothed as he fetched him up with a jerk. "Whoa." And he leaped on his back.

The pasture lay before them, but there was only one escape and Johnny turned the stallion to the gate. Paynim charged down on it, confidently gathering his hoofs for the jump. He crouched, and Lightfoot leaned forward. They were over, skimming the bars like a bird in full flight, and Paynim went thundering on. A gun roared behind them, a bullet smashed against the rocks, but Paynim had his head and the open trail called him. He rushed around the corner and was gone.

Chapter Seventeen

Through black shadows and garish moonlight Paynim went at a gallop, down the trail he knew so well—the glad trail to Toógahboth, where he could drink, and gambol on the lakebed. Or perhaps some new loyalty to the man who bestrode him steeled his gallant heart for the race. Perhaps he knew that death followed and that danger lay before him, and sniffed the battle from afar. It was bred in his blood to love the tumult and the shouting the yells of fighting men as they charged, and he took the trail gloriously until, near the portals, he slowed down with a warning snort.

Johnny Lightfoot had ridden free, the rope slack on Paynim's neck, but as a great patch of moonlight opened up through the gateway, he reined in and looked about. Below him, in a pit of blackness, lay the pool of the dry waterfall, where Morgan had set his deep blasts, and against the overhanging south wall he could see empty canisters strewn about. Morgan had loaded his holes, and the shattered wall above seemed ready to fall at a touch. Lightfoot listened and looked back—then at a touch of the spurs Paynim stepped off down the steep slope.

There was no retreat, and with a good horse under him Lightfoot felt his courage return. His gun and pistols were gone, but once out in the open he

was armed with more than guns. He had speed—
he was mounted on Paynim. Where the moon cast
deep shadows along the south bank of the wash,
the stallion trotted on, snorting softly. Then, at a
second and lower gateway, between banks of storm-
borne boulders, he halted and snorted louder.

The open wash stretched before them, piled high
on both sides with windrows of rocks and brush,
and among them, moving slowly, Johnny could see
a line of horsemen advancing toward the gateway.
He was cut off, and, if he whipped out, they would
ride in and head him. Discretion here was the better part of valor—he reined over and took shelter
behind a rock.

Out on the flat the riders had halted, the great
sand wash seemed empty, but, as he waited, Lightfoot saw a man's head bob up. They had dismounted and were coming on afoot. First one and
then another showed his head as he passed, keeping hidden behind the cutbank of the channel, and
out on the desert Johnny could hear distant voices
and the *clack* of iron-shod hoofs on the rocks. Val
Bodie's men were scouting out the gateway, and
soon the furtive forms came back. Then a long line
of horsemen came stringing up the wash and he
laid his hand on Paynim's nose.

Lightfoot set himself and waited, but just before
they reached him, the leaders came to a halt. Others
rode up from the rear—their muffled voices rose
louder until at last Val Bodie spoke out.

"Oh, hell," he cursed, "are you seeing ghosts,
too? How do you know the old codger is there?"

"I heard him," defended a voice. "When I first
went up there. I heard his horse coming . . . down
the trail at a gallop. . . ."

"Well, Hank, you go up there," ordered Bodie. "And don't come back till you know something. He can't shoot to kill in this moonlight. . . ."

"Oh, he can't, eh?" sneered Hank. "Well, you try him. I've been up there and seen his work . . . he's drilling holes under that gateway and loading them with dynamite. He's trying to toll us in so he can shoot the wall down on us. I don't want no lost mine at all!"

"Well, I do," retorted Bodie, "and I'm going to get it, too. It's the Lost Breyfogle . . . that's a cinch. There ain't no doubt that old whiskers is Frying-Pan George, and we know that he had the ore. Are you going to let one crazy old 'coon stand between you and a mountain of gold? He's shot two men already, so we'll be justified in shooting him and locating the mine for ourselves."

"I'm game to shoot him, all right," grumbled Boots. "What I'm skeered of is that he will shoot me. He done tried it, already, and come close enough. . . ."

"*Aw*, shut up!" broke in Bodie. "Is there any man here that's got nerve enough to go up this cañon? If I have to do it myself, I'll claim the whole mine. But the man that goes up there, gits half! The rest of you damned cow thieves can go back to your knitting. I'll divide with the man that kills George!"

He paused, and in the silence that followed Johnny heard the sound of hoof beats, up the cañon.

"There he comes!" yapped a voice. "That's the way he came before! Only now he's cussing to beat hell!"

"Shut up!" ordered Bodie, as the thunder of hoofs came nearer and Lightfoot took a last look back. Diana's father was coming. Above the *clatter* of the horse Johnny could hear the old man cursing, and into a patch of moonlight he saw him ride at full gallop, his white beard whipping in the wind. But it was not to avenge his wrongs on Val Bodie that he came, and Lightfoot swung low on his horse. Then with a yell he dashed out, charging straight at the startled night riders, who scattered without firing a shot. But, although they gave way, they turned to look as he passed, and Bodie spurred after him on Fly.

"That's the stallion, boys!" he shouted. "Head him off! Don't let him out! By grab, there's a man on him! Ride!"

He fired his pistol into the air to warn the men below, but the next moment a pandemonium of shooting broke loose as Morgan encountered the advance. Bullets were flying in every direction and horsemen went racing past, but Lightfoot swept on down the wide, sandy wash, passing horsemen who stood confused, leading the pack of pursuers. One by one as he came upon them, they reined out and gave him the trail, but when they heard the shouting and saw Bodie coming on Fly, they jumped in and joined the chase.

Down the long, winding wash, over boulders and through bushes, Paynim led them like a stag before hounds, but they crowded their horses, whipping and spurring to cut him off, and Johnny slapped Paynim hard. A storm of gravel flew up behind as the stallion responded, and the night riders began to shoot. Then they came out on the lakebed, and with a glorious burst of speed the thoroughbred pulled out in the lead. Straight as an arrow he flew, his head splitting the wind, his mane and tail floating away, and Johnny Lightfoot rose up, laughing.

The *playa* seemed flying past him while he sat still on the back of his noble horse. The sound of Paynim's hoof beats was like the rattle of a drum, drowning out the scattering pistol shots behind. They were free, and all the horses that Johnny had ridden were forgotten in his love for Paynim. Even when his enemies were left far behind, he let the stallion gallop on. There was nothing in the world but him and his mount, gliding out across a silvery sea.

A line of trees rose before him, and Johnny turned to the south, down the trail that led out of the valley, while Paynim, blowing hard and shaking his head, slowed down to a gentle trot.

"Good boy!" exulted Lightfoot, patting his neck again and again, and the foam-flecked stallion snorted forth his challenge as he gazed back into the night.

On the brow of the first hill Lightfoot stopped and listened. The *rattle* of rifle shots came dimly through the night, and Paynim pricked his ears, but no one followed behind. Spits of light stabbed the blackness at the mouth of the cañon. They were fighting for their mountain of gold—Val Bodie and his riders—and against them the half-crazed man known to them as Frying-Pan George.

Lightfoot sighed as he watched the distant fireflies that played about the mouth of Devil's Cañon. But for Diana and her horse he would be shut in there yet, or run to earth like a rabbit. He had escaped, but Diana was lost. Not an hour before they had watched the moon's rising while she had demanded her kiss. Then Paynim had snorted and across the stile her father had risen up, shooting. Shots, races, pursuits had crowded one upon the other—new terrors, new dangers, new escapes— and now he stood alone on the floor of the mighty valley and looked back where the fireflies played.

He was turning away to rub down Paynim's limbs when a flash lit up the sky. It was followed by a rumble and the deep *thud* of a blast. Then the cañon mouth was bathed anew in fire. It leaped up like the flare from the muzzle of a cannon, and there came a deep, earth-moving roar. The ground trembled again and with dull reverberations Light-foot heard the shattered wall fall. The gateway was closed—there was no way in or out. Diana was shut off from the world.

Chapter Eighteen

There was a low rumble in the air, the jostling of falling rocks as they came tumbling down from the shattered heights, and then with a last *thump* each found its lowest level and the desert stillness returned. Solemn mountains, rising high, made a black wall in the moonlight, and out across the flats Johnny Lightfoot could hear the wild burros, stampeding before the noise of the blasts. Enúpi Kai had claimed its own. The devil man had struck and the cañon's mouth had closed like a trap.

Lightfoot mounted and rode, his mind in a turmoil, hardly knowing which way he went, but at the entrance to the wash that led up to Daylight Spring, Paynim snorted and set his hoofs. Up that cañon, by Hole-in-the-Rock, as they rode out into the moonlight, twenty night riders had once swept down on them and led him back to Toógahboth, to be tied to a stake and starved. There was a menace in its dark shadows and Paynim drew back, turning his head down the Furnace Creek trail.

"What's the matter?" inquired Johnny, patting his neck solicitously. "Well, have your own way . . . that's a Jonah trail for both of us." And he reined away to the south.

The line of clay hills drew farther away and giant sand dunes loomed before them. Lost Valley fell behind, and, as dawn painted the east, they came to Esahbwoó, the Place of Death.

Paynim snorted and shied at the wreck of a huge wagon, rising up out of its covering of sand, and in the pale light of morning Lightfoot could see the marks of shovels where others had been half unearthed. The treasure hunters had been there, digging once more for the box of gold that legend said the emigrants had carried.

At the creek where Paynim's father, Selim, had given his master warning, Paynim snuffed the poison water and turned away. Then, with his nose to the wind, he followed the trail of the treasure hunters, and Lightfoot gave him his head.

There was fresh blood on Johnny's shirt where the jumping and riding had opened his half-healed wounds, and his throat was parched with thirst. But Captain Jack had warned him of the poisonous qualities of the water, and he spurred Paynim on toward the south.

Twenty miles down the valley, so Captain Jack had told him, there was a place called Enúpi Psoógobie, where a great stream of water gushed out. But they had avoided the spot, for the Shoshones often camped there, and Jack was a hunted man. He had stolen the daughter of Eatum-Up Jake, the fiercest warrior of the tribe, and the penalty for his crime was death. But Captain Jack was waiting for his master at Pahrump, and Lightfoot took the trail at a lope.

The sun rose, glaring over the peaks of the Funeral Range, and smote him with its torrid heat. Lightfoot found himself reeling as if from a blow and the wound on his head beat and throbbed. Then he caught at the saddle horn, for he felt himself falling, but Paynim jogged steadily on. The spell passed and Johnny looked up to see strange mountains at his left and at the base of a far hill-side he spied a spot of green, with the white of a spring at its base.

Paynim raised his head as if he smelled the distant water and lengthened his jog to a lope. He was tireless as an antelope and before an hour had passed he was drinking at Cow Springs. Johnny dropped out of his saddle and buried his face in the muddied pool. Then he drank and wet his head, and, while Paynim cropped the grass, he lay in the horse's shadow to escape the burning sun.

The first hot day of summer had come and the valley lay quivering in the heat. Mesquite trees danced ghost-like in the close-up mirage, and below him, like a vision of some distant desert scene, Lightfoot saw the green tips of three palms. He rose up and watched them closely, and at their feet he saw a house—a white house, with trees behind. Along a picket fence a horse was plodding—an old horse with long, stilt-like legs. It was the mirage, of course, turning the desert into a lake and lengthening the trunks of the trees. But the horse was real—he moved!

Lightfoot laid hold of his saddle horn and heaved himself up on his mount, and, as they jogged down the trail, he could see a group of Indians watching his progress from the top of a hill. Then at a turn of the path the house rose up before him, and a man was standing at the gate. Half concealed behind a post, he held a rifle across his arm, and Johnny reined in to a walk.

"Hello!" he hailed, raising his hand in the peace sign. But the stranger, watching him intently, did not respond.

As Lightfoot rode nearer, he saw a woman looking out through the door—a pretty woman with black hair combed smoothly back, and she bore a baby in her arms.

"Who are you and what's your business?" demanded the man peremptorily.

Johnny came to a halt. Many times before in that wild desert country, where both fugitives and outlaws sought shelter, he had been met by men waiting at the gate. This man was tall and stooping, with high cheek bones and level, piercing eyes—and Lightfoot knew he was on the dodge.

"My name's Lightfoot," he announced. "Johnny Lightfoot from Virginia City. I've had trouble, and I'm out of grub."

"Trouble with who?" inquired the stranger after a pause. "We have to be careful out here."

"With Val Bodie," responded Johnny. "He shot me in the back. We got tangled up over this horse."

"I've heard about you." The man nodded, beckoning him closer. "Is that one of those Night Water wild horses?"

"Sure is," answered Lightfoot. "But he's no more wild than I am. Look at that! He's gentle as a dog."

He dropped down and laid a hand on Paynim's nose, but the stallion did not flinch.

"Stranger, my name is Chatfield," spoke up the man behind the post. "Are you looking for anybody of that name?"

"Not me!" returned Lightfoot. "All I want is a little grub. And I've got the money to pay for it."

"Well, come in, then!" invited Chatfield, throwing open the gate. "And I'm sure glad to see that horse. If you don't know it already, I'll tell you right now . . . that's a thoroughbred Kentucky racer."

"I reckon you're right," agreed Johnny. "But that makes no difference. The horse is mine. I caught him."

"So I hear," responded Chatfield. "So the Indians tell me. But I had an uncle, Randolph Morgan, who perished up at Salt Creek, and I'll wager those horses were his."

"That was a long time ago," retorted Lightfoot. "Do you make any claim to this horse?"

"Oh, no," denied Chatfield. "But I knew Uncle Randolph's racers. Do you see those three black marks on the rump of this horse? Those are the direct hereditary markings, come down from Eclipse, the greatest thoroughbred stallion in England."

Lightfoot stopped short and brushed the hair out of his eyes, swollen half shut from riding bareheaded through the heat.

"Mister Chatfield," he said slowly, "I don't give a damn for those markings or your uncle Randolph. If you want one of his horses, go and ketch him the way I did. I'll fight for this horse."

"You don't need to," answered Chatfield shortly. "I don't claim him, and never did. But it certainly is remarkable to find those black marks on a horse that's been foaled in Death Valley."

"Now, listen," flared up Lightfoot, "and get this through your head right now. It's the law in this country that you can't claim a horse unless he bears your brand. If a horse is running wild on the open range, he belongs to the first man that ropes him. I roped this horse and I claim him, understand? It makes no difference where he came from!"

Chatfield gazed at him, glowering, his rifle in his hand, but before he could speak a woman's voice came to them—a gentle voice, but very firm.

"Jim," she said, "can't you see the man is sick? Don't keep him standing out in the sun!"

"No! Come in!" spoke up Chatfield. "And bring your horse in with you. Did you say Val Bodie shot you?"

"Four buckshot in my back. And I bumped my head ketching this horse. He dragged me off in the rocks."

"Well, come in, come in," invited Chatfield. "I'm sure glad Bodie didn't get your horse. He's a man I've got no use for, because I know he's a crook . . . and a cowardly, murdering crook at that!"

"Now, Jim," warned the woman reprovingly. "Mister Bodie never did us any harm."

"No, but he will," retorted Chatfield, "the first chance he gets. Well, all right!" And he led the way to the door. "Damaris," he said formally, "this is Mister . . . er . . . Lightfoot. Missus Chatfield, Mister Lightfoot."

"Glad to meet you," mumbled Johnny as she came down the steps and smilingly offered her hand. "I'm a hard-looking case, but. . . ."

"We'll take care of you," she said.

He felt her arm about him as he stumbled in through the doorway. Then in the coolness of the dark house his strength suddenly failed him and he sank down on a cot. He had traveled as far as his nerve could take him—far enough, for the woman was bending over him.

He awoke from a long sleep to hear a baby's thin wail and swift feet hurrying through the house.

Then the voice of the woman as she took up her child, every word a cooing caress. It was strange, in this wild country—and with a husband like hers—but Lightfoot listened, he smiled. But for her he would have stood bareheaded in the sun, until he fainted from weakness and pain. Now his bruised head was bandaged, a wet cloth lay over his eyes, and he felt his strength coming back.

But Chatfield was a fighter. He was hard.

Lightfoot took off the cloth and gazed about the room, and, as he stirred, Damaris's head appeared in the doorway, and she tiptoed over to his side.

"How are you feeling?" she asked, running her hand over his brow. "Would you like a glass of cool milk?"

"You bet ye . . . gimme two of them," responded Johnny. "I'm mighty nigh starved to death."

"Not too much at once," she advised him, smiling, as she brought in a pitcher and a glass. "How did you happen to lose your hat?"

"I forget"—he grinned—"whether Bodie shot it off or I lost it when my horse bumped my head. Sure needed it, too, this morning."

"It's getting hot," she said. "Nothing, though, to what it will be. It was a hundred and twenty-nine last August."

"Lord Almighty!" he exclaimed. "Were you here?"

"All summer." She sighed. "But the winters are wonderful. My husband has charge of the ranch."

"Ranch, eh?" he repeated. "What do you raise?"

"Oh, alfalfa . . . there's forty acres. And besides, he guards the water rights. The borax company claims the creek. But we're really here to hide . . .

like all the rest of them, I guess. That's why Jim was a little sharp at first."

"Oh, that's all right," responded Johnny. "You've more than made up for it. And my head was spinning like a top."

"I could see," she said, "your face going white. That's the way it affects them . . . before a stroke. So I just let you have a good sleep. But now, if you like, I'll get Jim and we'll doctor your back."

"Mighty kind of you," assented Lightfoot. "Is my horse all right? Keep him tied, or he'll start back home."

"Yes, Jim has taken care of him," she answered, and went out to call her husband in.

A blast of hot air, like the breath of a furnace, swept in as she opened the door, and Johnny could feel his head begin to spin. He had had a touch of heat. But as the door was closed, a moist coolness rose up from the sprinkled earth of the floor. Despite the hot wind they kept their house comfortable—but what a place for a woman to live!

She came back, still smiling, and above her in saturnine calm her husband gazed down on their guest. He was over six feet tall, with the stoop of hard work in his powerful shoulders, but still a young man in his prime.

"Let me see your back," he said. And then with practiced hand he followed the course of each buckshot. "You're all right," he grunted. "No lead in you now. How many days ago were you shot?"

"Oh, four or five," ventured Johnny. "I've been hiding out in a cave."

"Mighty lucky," observed Chatfield, "to have that arnica with you. Damaris, fetch me out the balsam."

He cleaned up the wounds and poured on a fragrant balsam that smelled of myrrh and aromatic herbs, but Lightfoot knew from the grim silence he kept that his mind was still on the horse. Had he come here from Kentucky to seek the priceless thoroughbreds that his uncle had brought so far? Or was he, too, a fugitive from that terrible feud that had driven Randolph Morgan from his home?

Johnny meditated as he lay there, accepting favors from his hand, whether Chatfield had a claim on Paynim. For the horse was not a broomtail but a pedigreed stallion. Lightfoot had taken him—no, stolen him—from Morgan. But Randolph Morgan was buried from the world as surely as if he were dead. And for twenty years he had been counted dead, disguised as Frying-Pan George. The horse was not Chatfield's, in any case, as long as his uncle still lived. He was Johnny's to have and to hold until Devil's Cañon gave up its living dead. Even then he would not be Chatfield's, for Diana was Morgan's daughter.

"Mister Chatfield," he began at last, "what's this about your uncle? Did you come out here to look for his horses?"

"I came out here," replied Chatfield, "to get away from a feud. You might have heard of the Chatfield-Tolliver war. But the reason I came here, instead of somewhere else, was to find out the truth about my uncle. He was a man of wealth, and, when he left the Bluegrass country, he took with him a box of money and jewels. These jewels, according to what I can learn from the Indians, have never been recovered from the wagons, which meantime have been buried by the sand. So at intervals I've been digging in the sand dunes at Salt Creek . . . you might have noticed it when you came past."

"Yes, I did," admitted Lightfoot. "And I've noticed something else. These Shoshones won't talk about that fight. They've got something on their conscience, because they looted those wagons. Maybe they've got the jewels hidden out."

"More than likely," grumbled Chatfield. "But seeing that wild stallion has settled my mind on one point. My uncle Randolph died here. How many more horses are there up there?"

"Well . . . ten," answered Lightfoot. "But there's no use of you hunting them. There ain't a horse in this country can ketch 'em."

"Then how did you catch yours?" demanded Chatfield.

Lightfoot saw Damaris in the door. "Well," he began, "it's quite a long story. But I roped him at the water hole by moonlight."

"Oh, Jim," spoke up his wife, "there's somebody coming. Panamint Tom is signaling from the hill."

For a moment Chatfield hesitated, eager to go on with his questioning. Then he rose up and grabbed his gun.

"It's Bodie," he said, after a long look out the door.

Johnny leaped up like a flash. "Lend me a rifle!" he clamored as he ran out on the porch. "He's after me . . . and my horse!"

"You don't need a rifle," answered Chatfield quietly. "You're our guest, Mister Lightfoot . . . I'll attend to Val Bodie myself."

He strode out to the gate and without a word of warning raised his gun to his shoulder and fired. The bullet struck up the dust in front of a galloping horseman, and Lightfoot recognized Bodie. He was mounted on Fly, and far down the road Johnny could see six other night riders. They had followed on his trail after their defeat at the gateway, wild with anger and the lust to kill. For once more, from under their noses, he had carried off the golden stallion, and Bodie was out for revenge.

At the puff of dust Bodie threw up one hand, but came on, making the peace sign. Once more, and with the same unhurried precision, Jim Chatfield raised his rifle, and the bullet struck almost at the hoofs of the man's horse. Bodie reined in abruptly, holding his hand up for a talk, turning to look back impatiently for his men, and, as they spurred up behind him, he jumped his horse into a gallop. But the big gun spoke again.

Bodie ducked as if he were shot and the men who rode behind him swung down along their horses' necks. Then they stopped and Bodie began to shout. But Chatfield, without listening, stepped out from behind his post and motioned them imperiously away. Bodie looked about wildly—at the Indians on the hill and the lone man with a rifle on his arm. Then he reined away abruptly and galloped off down the road, while Chatfield paced back to the house.

"I know jest how to handle that kind of folks," he said. "Learned it early, back home in Kaintuck."

Chapter Nineteen

"Jim Chatfield!" cried his wife. "What in the world do you mean, shooting at Bodie without making a sign? Haven't we had troubles enough without your beginning all over again and starting another feud?"

"Oh, shore, shore, now, Damaris," he replied good-naturedly as he shoved three more cartridges into his magazine. "It's all right . . . there's no harm done. If I'd let 'em come closer, they'd've started a fight, and then I'd've had to kill someone. And if they had come to the gate, they'd've demanded Mister Lightfoot, and I wouldn't give him up no-how."

"I sure want to thank you, Mister Chatfield," spoke up Johnny Lightfoot. "Because there's no doubt they had come to get me. But I certainly hope," he added with a glance at Damaris, "that I haven't brought down trouble on your home."

"None in the world!" declared Chatfield with an easy smile. "This man Bodie has been pestering me and I'm right glad we had a showdown. Now he'll know right where to find me."

"Now, Jim," reproached his wife, "you know very well you just did that to start another war. I declare, it's in the blood. I never knew a Chatfield that wouldn't pick a fight, if he could!"

"The same to you." Chatfield grinned. "Ain't you a fighting Tolliver? I was sure a lucky man to win you for my wife with that tribe of warriors on my trail."

He put his arm about her waist and drew her down beside him, and now his hard face was suddenly illuminated by a kind and rugged smile.

"That's why I loved you so," he went on soothingly. "There's no coward blood in your veins. The Tollivers are all fighters, and I'm a fighter myself. When I tell a man to stop, he wants to stop."

"Yes, but Jim!" she sobbed. "You never made a sign. You never even lifted a hand. Think of our baby in there! And what would become of us if these ruffians of Bodie's should kill you?"

"They won't kill me," he answered confidently. "I never felt so safe in my life. Those Indians are better than watchdogs, and no man can pass that gate without asking for my consent. And another thing, sweetheart . . . I looked that gang over, and the man behind Bodie was Riley Sloper."

"Riley Sloper!" she cried. "Oh, Jim, they've found us! They'll all come here now . . . the whole clan!"

"No, they won't," he comforted. "It's too far away. I could have killed Riley, but, just for your sake, I sent the bullet past his ear."

"Oh, Jim!" she burst out, laying her head against his breast. "I'm afraid. Don't you go outside the fence!"

"No, I won't, darling," he promised, "until the hot weather comes on. Then they'll all go away. The whole gang!"

"Oh, I wish it would get hot, then." She sighed.

Lightfoot cleared his throat. "Seems to me," he suggested, "not to contradict anybody, it's pretty near hot already."

"You're not used to it," returned Chatfield, giving

his wife a kiss and sending her into the house. "It's only jest beginning to get warm. Wait till the south wind blows up and the sandstorms come in and the water in the salt marshes boils. Yes, suh, boils! I've seen it myself. And why shouldn't it, I'd like to ask, when it's a hundred and thirty in the shade and water boils at two hundred and twelve? There's only a few degrees difference . . . and the more salt you put into your water, the quicker the pot will sing."

"Yes, but how do you live?" demanded Lightfoot.

"Oh, we live." Chatfield shrugged. "Lots of water, running right past. Come over here and I'll show you my fan. The old flywheel off of an engine . . . I run it by waterpower. That's really what keeps us alive."

He led the way to a long corridor, between the two mud houses that were ensconced beneath a double roof. As he lifted a gate, the rushing ditch was turned aside, sending its waters over a miniature mill wheel. The flume filled, the paddles turned, and with a thrashing beat the flywheel started its fan. Splashing water wet the wings as they went whistling past, and down the narrow hallway a cool wind stirred the dust until Chatfield sprinkled water on the floor.

"In front of that," he said, "with a wet sheet for a cover, you could outlive a blast from hell. And when people are hunted as Damaris and I have been, we're glad when the hot weather comes. Even the Shoshones quit us and go up on the peaks. We're alone for months at a time. That's why we stay here. We're safe."

Lightfoot nodded silently, taking his stand in the

cool draft that sucked down the dampened corridor, and Damaris came out of her room.

"Here's why we stay." She smiled, holding up a cooing baby. "This is young Jim ... otherwise, James Tolliver Chatfield."

"I see," responded Johnny. "You've done called the feud off, eh?"

"Yes." Jim nodded. "But the Tollivers haven't. You see, we couldn't be married on account of the feud, so. . . ."

"So he rode over and stole me," ended Damaris. And she cast a proud glance at her husband.

"Yes, I'll have to admit it," confessed Chatfield. "But I just had to have her, that's all."

"I've never regretted it," said Damaris. "How could I, with little Jim and all? But if Bodie should come back and. . . ."

"You can count on me," spoke up Lightfoot impulsively. "I'm only one man, but if the kid here needs my services. . . ."

He held out one finger and little Jim laid hold of it, while his parents exchanged glances and smiled.

"I'll shake on that, too," announced Chatfield.

"You took me in," said Johnny, "and I stay by my friends. But, say, I've got something to tell you."

He sat down in the cool corridor and told them briefly of Randolph Morgan. And last of all he mentioned Diana.

"Oho!" exclaimed Chatfield. "So that's who took care of you while you were hiding out in that cave."

"Yes," admitted Lightfoot, "it was Diana who took care of me. And to tell you the truth, it was Diana who found me and smuggled me up the cañon. But when her old man discovered us there. . . ."

"You fell in love with her!" charged Damaris impulsively.

"Yes . . . and her father tried to kill me," responded Johnny. "I might as well tell you the whole of it."

"Oh, Jim," Damaris breathed, leaning her head against her husband and gazing up into his eyes. "Isn't it wonderful? Shut up all her life in that cañon, and then to have him come by. Was she afraid?" she demanded eagerly. "Why, she'd never even seen a young man."

"Now, darling," protested her husband, "isn't this getting kinder personal?"

"No, that's all right." Lightfoot smiled. "You folks are her cousins and you're entitled to know the truth. Diana was afraid . . . at first. But after we became acquainted . . . well, of course, she'd been very lonely, especially since her mother's death. Her father undoubtedly is insane."

"Yes, but why did he try to kill you?" persisted Damaris.

"Well, he found us together," answered Lightfoot shortly, "sitting out in the moonlight, watching the horses. We were up on the stile, and I'd just saddled Paynim . . . when I saw his rifle shoved out toward me. I ducked and it went off, right over my head, so there's no doubt about his intentions. But Diana grabbed the gun and I jumped Paynim over the bars. . . ."

"So that's the way you got him," spoke up Chatfield.

"That's the way," agreed Johnny. "And if you want to call it stealing or. . . ."

"No, no, the horse is yours. But I thought you said at first. . . ."

"I said I roped him." Lightfoot nodded. "And I did. I'm the first man to ketch one of those Night Water horses, but Val Bodie took him away from me. Then, when I went down to steal him back, Diana rode in on us and Bodie caught her horse, too. It would take all day to explain the rest of the mix-up. But when we got through, I'd turned both horses loose and stopped a load of buckshot to boot."

"And Diana escaped!" thrilled Damaris. "Then she found you and carried you home."

"But unfortunately," continued Johnny, "her father had sworn that he'd kill the first man he caught there. He's got a rich mine and he's afraid somebody will steal it. . . ."

"Oh, so that's why he tried to kill you?"

"Reckon so," grunted Lightfoot. "Didn't stop to ask no questions. So here I am . . . horse and all."

"And are you planning," Damaris asked roguishly, "to go back and rescue Diana? Uncle Randolph will be watching for you now."

"I didn't tell you," replied Lightfoot, "but right after I left, he blew up the entrance to the cañon. Shot the walls down and closed the gateway . . . you could feel the blast for miles. So I'm afraid I can't get back."

"Why, Jim!" she cried. "Uncle Randolph must be crazy. Can't you go up and help her, honey?"

"You don't need to," interposed Johnny, "while I'm on the job. And if anyone can get her out, I can. But in case I do get in there and rescue Diana, can I count on you folks to take care of her? Because, to tell you the truth, she wanted to come out with me. Only, of course, there was no place to go."

"Why, certainly!" exclaimed Damaris. "Just think

of the poor child, and no one but him to turn to. Is she pretty, Mister Lightfoot? Is she? Honest?"

"She's too pretty," responded Johnny. "That's what I'm afraid of."

Damaris exchanged glances with her husband. "Well, you bring her right here," she answered demurely. "And Mister Lightfoot, you're a very nice man."

Chapter Twenty

Johnny Lightfoot awoke at daylight to hear a woman singing. It was Damaris, humming while she worked. The heat of the day had passed, and the long, sweltering night, and she was up about her tasks at dawn. What was it, he wondered, that made her heart so glad at the bottom of this sinkhole of hell? With death so near at hand, what had she to sing for? And yet, as he listened, she sang on.

Not for many a year had he heard a woman singing. There was something about her voice that reminded him of Diana, when she, too, had awakened to love. He had not forgotten the clinging touch of her arms, the child-like kisses on his cheeks, the raptures of delight with which she greeted him in the dusk. But it was her secret—he would guard it well. No one in the days to come, if he saved her from her imprisonment, should mention it to her shame. She was his, to take care of and protect.

He tiptoed out on the porch and looked back up the long road. Val Bodie would be watching for him now. Past the door, in a wide ditch, a brawling stream of water flowed down from the cañon above, and along its banks he could see the *ranchería* where the Shoshones made their camps. These were Captain Jack's people, but they seemed to know Horse-Ketchum, for they avoided him with sullen looks. Yet little that happened escaped their eyes; they were watching him now from the distance.

Johnny felt of his lame back to see if he could ride, and went out to Paynim's corral. Here at least the stallion was safe, for Chatfield had built a stockade of mesquite posts with no entrance but the gate in front. It surrounded his house like the outworks of a fort—and Jim, too, was up with the dawn. A forkful of hay came over the fence from the stack on the other side, but Paynim raised his head after he had seized the first mouthful and gazed at his master anxiously.

"No, Paynim," said Lightfoot, "we're not going home today. I've got to go to Pahrump and find my Indian friend, and you're too danged good-looking, old horse. You're like a pretty woman . . . you'd just get me into trouble." He patted him on the neck.

"I'll stake you to a horse!" shouted Chatfield over the fence. "And a good horse, too, Mister Lightfoot. You just leave Paynim here and, when you go to Pahrump, bring me back a box of cartridges."

"I'll bring you back ten boxes," promised Johnny, "if you'll keep Bodie from stealing Paynim."

That evening after dark he rode up Furnace Creek on Chatfield's rangy roan. Chatfield had also given him loan of a six-gun. Hour after hour he kept on up the gravelly wash until, crossing the summit, he saw the pale quarter moon, rising belatedly over the desert. He was up out of the sink, on the broad reaches of the Amargosa whose bitter waters in time of flood swept south of the Funeral Range and back into Death Valley itself. It was a country that Lightfoot knew, for Captain Jack had led him through it when they were hiding their trail from the night riders.

As daylight approached, he rode in toward Shoshone, to take shelter in its thickets of mesquite. But as he circled the point and headed up toward the spring, he came upon his own mules, feeding.

For a moment, despite their brands, Johnny doubted his own eyes. Yet here were his pack mules, hobbled, and in the distance he could see Captain Jack's horse. He even recognized, among the mesquite trees, the top of his own tent. But he had told Jack to wait for him at Pahrump.

Lightfoot quit the trail and took cover among the screw beans, and, as he spurred on, his anger grew. While he had been fighting lone-handed against Bodie, Captain Jack had seized the occasion to decamp with his mules and supplies.

The tent was set back in the midst of the thicket at the end of a narrow path, and, when Lightfoot saw his coffee pot on the stones of an Indian fire, he reined in and drew his gun.

"Hello!" he hailed.

From the door of the tent a woman stared out at him, wondering. She was a Paiute, and not uncomely, with a clean dress and her hair neatly banged. For an instant she stood at gaze. Then, seeing a white man, she dived under the tent and fled through the brush like a rabbit. Lightfoot looked around at the old, familiar things—his butcher knife, his hatchet, his rawhide packs—and at sight of his own bed spread out in the tent he let out a louder yell.

"Jack!" he shouted. "Where are you . . . you damned rascal? Come out of that brush! This is Horse-Ketchum!"

"Ho! H'lo!" responded a voice from the depths of the thicket, and Captain Jack gazed out at him furtively.

"What the devil do you mean," demanded Lightfoot indignantly, "running off with my outfit and mules? Come out of there, dog-gone it, or I'll shoot you!"

"No! No shootum!" protested Jack, stepping out into the open. "Wha's matter? Me thinkum you dead."

Captain Jack was nattily attired in Lightfoot's own cartridge belt, tailored town pants, blue shirt, and silk handkerchief. Only the wire-haired head and the startled, beady eyes kept the disguise from being complete. But Captain Jack was frightened— he was trembling.

"Ho! H'lo!" he greeted again, advancing with a doubtful smile. "You Horse-Ketchum? Where you been?"

"None of your damned business!" burst out Lightfoot angrily. "Why the hell didn't you go to Pahrump, like I told you? And you've sure got a nerve, putting on my best clothes. Dog-gone you, Jack, I ought to kill you!"

"No! No killum," entreated the Indian apologetically. "Everybody say . . . 'Horse-Ketchum, she dead.' Me see Bodie ride your horse. Me see Pete Boots wear your hat. No come back . . . me thinkum dead."

"Like hell!" railed Johnny. "Who's that woman that ran away?"

"My wife," announced Captain Jack. "Me ketchum 'nother woman. Paiute woman . . . good squaw."

"Yes, but that don't give you license to give her

my blankets and set her up in housekeeping in my tent. You can keep the outfit now and I'll buy me another one. How much of that money have you got left?"

"All gone!" answered Captain Jack dolefully.

"What? The whole five hundred? What'd you do with it, Jack? You owe me for this outfit, savvy?"

"Money gone," repeated Jack. "Me buyum squaw . . . Ash Meadows. Good woman . . . he costum four horses. Then . . . well, buyum grub, givum feast. Everybody git drunk. Pretty soon money all gone."

"Hell's bells," grumbled Lightfoot, surveying his purloined outfit. "Well, Jack, you can work it out."

"No," objected the Indian. "Me ketchum woman now."

"No difference," responded Johnny. "You stole my outfit, savvy? You know what the Hiko man does when he ketches an Indian stealing!"

He wrapped his finger around his neck and made a motion up and Captain Jack saw a new light.

"You go back . . . ketchum horse?" he inquired. "My wife, he go, too. Good cook."

"You send your wife home to her people," ordered Lightfoot. "Give her grub, give her blankets, give her everything you stole. But I don't want a woman along."

"Where you go?" repeated Captain Jack. "Too hot Death Valley now."

"Too hot for woman," answered Johnny grimly. "You send her back to Ash Meadows."

"Me 'fraid!" came out Jack. "Maybeso Shoshones kill me. Eatum-Up Jake . . . she mad. Me buyum Paiute woman. Shoshones all mad . . . maybe killum."

"Now here," said Lightfoot, "I'll take care of the Shoshones. You're with me, savvy, and I need you in my business. I won't let anybody kill you."

"All right, me go," agreed Captain Jack. And then he glanced up at Lightfoot slyly. "You go back . . . ketchum horse?" he asked.

"No, Jack." Johnny grinned. "I'm going to steal me a woman. You come along and help, and, when we get through. . . ."

"What woman?" Jack demanded eagerly.

"Never mind," said Lightfoot. "You know the devil man at Night Water? Maybeso we steal his girl."

"No *wano!*" grunted Captain Jack.

But Johnny regarded him sternly. "I know what I want," he said. "You ain't called in for an opinion on this at all, you old rascal. You know the ghost maiden that used to ride the moon's horses? All right, we're going to steal her."

"No good," repeated Captain Jack stubbornly, and then his sly grin returned. "How much you pay me?" he asked.

"I'll pay you one hundred dollars . . . and all this stuff you stole."

"All right," answered Jack. "Me go."

Chapter Twenty-one

The trail to Mormon Lake was crowded with prospectors as Johnny Lightfoot and Captain Jack rode out of Pahrump. The name on every lip, the magic word that lured them on, was Breyfogle. The lost Breyfogle Mine had been found! Lightfoot listened curiously, hardly believing his ears, to the rumors of the strike, and then it came over him that he himself had seen the treasure. The rush was to Devil's Mountain.

As they neared Daylight Pass, the stampede reached its height. Men threw away their blankets, their provisions, even their water kegs, in order to be the first on the grounds. They traveled day and night, flailing their reluctant animals on until at Hole-in-the-Rock they met the tide setting back, and all the rumors fell flat.

"It's a fake!" yelled the boomers as they came dragging into camp. "Go back, you damned fools, before you perish with the heat. It's another one of Bodie's tricks."

But the stampeders never wavered. They poured on down the cañon until they came to Night Water, where numerous men were camped under the trees. And with them, leading the van, went Lightfoot and Captain Jack, for Val Bodie had disappeared. He it was who had spread the rumors of treasure trove, showing the sacks of rich ore he had bought from Frying-Pan George, exhibiting

Johnny's Breyfogle rock. But when the leaders of the rush fought their way to Devil's Mountain, they found the entrance to the cañon blocked.

A wall of loose rock 100 feet high dammed the way to the fabled bonanza, and up on the cliffs Frying-Pan George was standing guard, ready to shoot any man who approached. It was then the rumor spread that Val Bodie had started the rush in order to bring trade to his store. Coming and going through Mormon Lake, the stampeders had spent their money on whiskey at two bits a drink, but when the first rumors of a fake sprang up, Bodie had ridden off, no one knew where. All they knew was that with him he had taken the Breyfogle gold—and the gold that had been spent over the bar.

Lightfoot camped at Night Water, where not a month before he had rescued Diana from the clutches of Bodie. Now she and her horses were shut up in the cañon, and across the entrance there was a wall of crumbling rock. Through his glasses he could see the raw scar along the cliff where the towering mass of stone had come down. But, although he scanned the bench above, nothing stirred on the look-out point, and at sundown he rode up closer.

At the mouth of the cañon, blocks of rock had come tumbling down, but below them, where once the waterfall had been, there was a wall of solid stone. Randolph Morgan's first blast had shot out the inclined slope, and the second blast had brought down the cliff. There was no way up to the mass of shattered rock that hung at a balance above. How could one hope to surmount that dizzy pile, where every piece seemed tottering to its fall?

Lightfoot stood in the gathering dusk and gazed up at it grimly. Morgan was crazy, of course, but there was a method in his madness, for with two shots of powder he had shut his enemies out, and his horses and gold mine in. His cave was stored with provisions, the mountain sheep would supply his meat, and, whenever he became weary of his complete isolation, he could blast the cañon mouth clear.

Johnny called, but no one answered, and he went back to Night Water, where the stampeders had plans of their own.

Others had tried and failed, but in the morning they rode up to essay the solid barricade. Behind it lay the Breyfogle, greatest of all the storied mines that had made Death Valley famous, and, as they lined up before it, they discussed their scheme for blasting the obstruction away. Given the time and the powder, the cañon entrance could be cleared.

While they scanned the gateway, Lightfoot watched the heights where Frying-Pan George stood guard. A head appeared over the rampart and a gun barrel flashed. Then, balanced fearlessly on the brow of the cliff, the old man waved his rifle.

"Get away from there, you scoundrels!" he bellowed. And like one man the stampeders obeyed. But as they spurred back out of range, Johnny turned and watched the crags, waving his hand as a signal for Diana. Had he murdered her in his rage, this crack-brained old reprobate who stood menacing them still with his rifle?

Lightfoot reined in and shouted her name, while the rest whipped away, but his only answer was a shot from the cliff. Morgan had recognized his enemy and sensed the errand that brought him there, for the bullets came thick and fast. But as the shooting began, Johnny spied a silvery fox running away over a pile of rocks. And beneath, peeping out from among the boulders, he saw Diana's golden head.

Then a bullet came too close and his horse snorted and whirled. He waved his hat and fled, but his heart was glad. Diana lived, and she knew that her lover had come back for her. But he could not save her now, for to fetch her from that cañon, even if he could enter it, he would have to kill her father. It was better to wait, and come back.

All day the terrific heat beat down on their camp, while a wind out of the sink snatched up gravel and silt and buried them deep in sand. It came laden with the stench of steaming marshes and of acrid, sun-smitten greasewood, a smell such as Lightfoot had never sensed before—the rank breath of Death Valley in the heat. Wailing and grumbling while they waited for the sandstorm to lull, for the sun to sink at last behind the mountains, the prospectors at Night Water called down a thousand curses upon the author of their plight.

Val Bodie it was who, to gain a few dirty dollars, had brought them to this sinkhole of hell, but they swore, one and all, to raze his store to the ground if they ever escaped alive. So they lay, panting like lizards in the thin shade of the mesquite trees, until the long day came to a close, and, as a cool night wind sucked in from the high ground, Lightfoot rode off with the rest. But where the others turned off toward Daylight Pass, Lightfoot kept on south toward Furnace Creek Ranch, where Jim Chatfield would be awaiting his aid.

Val Bodie was desperate now, and, to avenge a fancied wrong, he was capable of any mischief. He held to the outlaws' code, and Jim Chatfield had humiliated him, turning him back before all his followers who so often he had rebuked for their faintheartedness. Chatfield had deprived him of his revenge when he had followed on Lightfoot's trail, and, more than that, Jim had deprived him of Paynim. It was that loss, most of all, that had roused Bodie's rancor, and Lightfoot knew he would come back.

The Stygian gloom of a desert night had settled down over Death Valley, as if the darkness, like a river, had drained down into its black depths, making the trail invisible to a horse. Captain Jack rode in the lead, driving the pack mules before him. Lightfoot was deep in thought. And when they were on the salt meadows by Esahbwoó, where the emigrants had perished, a horse neighed, loud and clear. Captain Jack's pony answered, the mules added their brays, and then out of the darkness, leaping and fighting against his hobbies, High Behind came crow-hopping up.

Lightfoot knew him first, recognizing his neigh, and swung down to cut the animal loose.

"Somebody come!" warned Jack as sudden voices were heard.

Lightfoot grabbed High Behind by the mane. Then, feeling his way down his forelegs, he slashed off the heavy hobbles and leaped up on Chatfield's horse.

"Who is that?" challenged a voice, and Jack turned the horses away. It was Val Bodie—he was digging out the wagons.

"Go to the devil!" taunted Johnny, throwing

High Behind into the bunch. And as Bodie began to shout, they took the back trail at a gallop, then turned off and made for the hills. The black night swallowed them up and they halted in a swale as a band of horsemen loped north. Then, quietly, they headed south, with High Behind trotting free, and never stopped till they came to the ranch.

From the top of the look-out hill a high yell roused the house and brought Chatfield to the gate with his gun. But Lightfoot rode up, laughing, reaching over to slap old High Behind, who responded with a playful kick. He had turned another trick on the unlucky Val Bodie and stolen back his captured horse. No small prize in itself, for High Behind was a racer and a range-toughened mustang to boot.

"Look what I've got!" he called. "My old mustang chaser, High Behind, the horse that Bodie stole! And this is my pard, Captain Jack."

"Drive 'em in," responded Chatfield. "And send the Injun up the ditch. I don't allow 'em inside the fence."

"Not any of 'em?" pleaded Lightfoot. "Jack's a mighty good Indian and. . . ."

"No Injuns!" answered Chatfield shortly.

Captain Jack rolled his frightened eyes.

"No, but listen," began Johnny as he saw the Shoshones advancing in a body down the ditch, "he's had trouble with Eatum-Up Jake. . . ."

"I don't give a damn," broke in Chatfield harshly. "No Injun passes that gate. Understand?"

His face, which had been so friendly, was drawn down in angry lines and his jaw was set like a steel trap.

"Yeah! Sure I understand!" answered Lightfoot angrily. He turned the horses back from the entrance.

"What's the matter?" cried Damaris, running down to the gate with little Jim still in her arms. "Oh, Jim, Mister Lightfoot is our friend!"

"I don't care!" flared back Chatfield. "He can't dictate to me. That's my rule. No Injuns inside the gate."

"Then I'll just camp outside," answered Johnny. "Come on, Jack. And don't you be scared."

He rode around the pack mules and drove them over to a mesquite tree that stood on the bank of the ditch, and Captain Jack followed in a daze. First he glanced at Horse-Ketchum, then at the crowd of jabbering Shoshones. At sight of Panamint Tom, the war chief, he dropped off and fell flat on the ground with his hands up over his head. For he had stolen a Shoshone woman, and the punishment for his crime was death.

Panamint Tom strode over toward him, leaving the rabble behind, and gave him a kick in the ribs.

"This Shoshone country!" he said in English for the benefit of Horse-Ketchum. "All this side of them mountains"—he pointed to the Funeral Range—"Shoshone country! This Injun Paiute!"

He grunted contemptuously and gave Jack another kick, but the latter only groveled at his feet. Then, in a long and impassioned speech, pointing often to the mountains and thrusting out his lips at Jack, the war chief harangued his people. By the pantomime alone, and the few words he understood, Lightfoot could follow the tale of Captain Jack's treachery to the tribe. He acted out the theft of the pretty Shoshone girl, and, as he went on to describe her distress and ultimate death, shouts of anger went up from the crowd.

They were swart men with high cheek bones and the bold eyes of their forefathers, the war-like Shoshones of the north, but Panamint Tom himself stood head and shoulders above them all, and he advanced upon Captain Jack threateningly.

"No *wano!*" he declaimed, giving the culprit another buffet while he glanced first at Lightfoot and then at Chatfield. "Bad Injun . . . stealum woman. Shoshone people killum. Me killum!" And he reached for his knife.

But Lightfoot stepped to the front. "This is Horse-Ketchum's pard," he stated. "You leave him alone. I hired him to help me ketch horses."

He faced the Indians calmly, and once more Panamint Tom glanced over at the face of his boss. But Jim Chatfield stood grimly silent, although his wife was clinging to his arm, and the war chief turned back arrogantly.

"This Shoshone country," he said again, pointing his hand toward the eastern mountains. "Paiute Injun come over . . . we killum. Shoshone go over . . . Paiute killum." He nodded, and reached for his knife.

"Here now, listen," spoke up Horse-Ketchum with a good-natured smile. "This man is my pard. Understand? Maybeso him Paiute . . . maybeso him Shoshone. No difference. He works for me."

"No *wano!*" shouted the war chief. "This man stealum woman. Good woman . . . b'long Eatum-Up Jake!"

He waved his hand toward a gaunt and evil-eyed savage who had been yapping on the edge of

the crowd, and with a yell of defiance Eatum-Up
Jake leaped forward, a long knife clutched in his
hand. His drawn face was working fiercely and
there was murder in his eye, but when Horse-
Ketchum stepped toward him, he stopped.

"Now here," warned Lightfoot, and one hand
touched his gun. "You put up that knife before my
pistol goes off and another bad Injun bites the dust.
You leave this man alone, understand?"

"No *wano!*" shrilled Eatum-Up Jake, making a
futile kick at Jack. "She steal my girl. Me killum!"

"No, you won't," contradicted Horse-Ketchum.
"How much you want for your girl?"

A subtle change came over the countenance of
the outraged father, and he turned exultantly to
the crowd. They shouted in great excitement and
Eatum-Up Jake shouted back. Then he turned and
spoke to Horse-Ketchum.

"Four horses!" he said succinctly.

"Two!" offered Johnny, suddenly flashing up
two fingers.

The whole crowd joined in on the haggling.
Hands went up and fingers were raised—some
clamoring for four, some for three—and Horse-
Ketchum unlashed a pack. From within he lifted
out a big sack of flour, a can of coffee, a bag of
sugar, and two plugs of trade tobacco. He laid them
on the ground and pointed to Captain Jack, then
held up two fingers again.

Once more in a clamor of shouting the clansmen
argued and gesticulated, but Panamint Tom stood
unmoved. He was their chief and he withheld his
voice.

"Here!" spoke up Horse-Ketchum, offering a
sack of tobacco and a block of matches for additional

incentive, and the chief of the Shoshones unbent. He rolled a cigarette, while Lightfoot rolled another, and passed the sack of makings through the crowd. Then, as the smoke drifted up and Horse-Ketchum flashed two fingers, the people shouted acclaim. Panamint Tom nodded gravely, Eatum-Up Jake accepted the presents—and Captain Jack rose up, ransomed.

Chapter Twenty-two

A big feast was on in the camp of the Shoshones when a yell rose up from the look-out on the hill, and Jim Chatfield came out to the gate. Since the quarrel over Captain Jack he had not spoken to Lightfoot, who was camped out under the trees, but after a brief glance up the road, Jim strode out, and Johnny saw that his anger had passed.

"You'd better come inside the fence," Chatfield said. "That's Bodie again . . . on your trail."

"Much obliged," answered Lightfoot, "but I'm not scared of him a bit."

"Well, bring the Injun with you," broke in Chatfield gruffly.

Captain Jack threw the packs on the mules and the lash ropes were tied. Then horses and mules alike were rushed through the gateway, while Jack looked back and laughed. His life had been spared at the intercession of Lightfoot, but the Shoshones had bristled like angry dogs when he had passed, and Eatum-Up Jake had snarled balefully. But now, inside the gate, he was safe from them all—and Bodie had halted up the road.

"Reckon he's looking for High Behind," suggested Johnny exultantly. "Every time that whelp steals anything, I steal it right back from him. He was digging around your wagons when I passed."

"Oh, he was, eh?" exclaimed Chatfield, and then he nodded grimly. "I know what's biting him," he said. "One of the Injuns, when we were digging there, found a fine gold watch. They're trying to locate that treasure box."

"He's afraid," jeered Lightfoot, stepping out into the open where Bodie and his men could see him. "He's on the dodge himself, and, if those stampeders ever catch him, they'll hang him for a certainty. So I suppose he's come down to lift my scalp."

"No, he's after mine," stated Chatfield. "Did you bring back those cartridges? Well, you've saved my bacon, because there's Riley Sloper. And Riley is a clean-strain killer."

He pronounced the words calmly, almost as if they were words of praise, and Lightfoot saw in the level glance of Chatfield's eyes that he, too, was a killer, and proud of it.

"Riley is after me," Chatfield continued impersonally. "He's Dad Tolliver's right-hand man, sent out to track me down. And according to the code he can't go back until he kills me, or I get him. But Mister Lightfoot, I hate to kill him . . . because Damaris is a Tolliver. So I'm going to wait for the heat."

"Wait?" echoed Lightfoot. "My Lord, ain't this hot enough?"

"You wait till July," returned Chatfield, "and every fly on this ranch will drop dead. They gather under the leaves on the north side of the house and fall to the ground in windrows. That's heat . . . the kind that kills people. And I don't reckon Riley can stand it."

"Well, I can," asserted Johnny. "I've got to stay, Jim, because, Bodie or no Bodie, I'm going back to get Diana."

"You won't leave this ranch for a month," predicted Chatfield as the night riders rode back up the road. "Those rascals have gone back to camp at Cow Springs. They'll be watching us night and day."

"Let 'em watch," answered Lightfoot. "I'll sneak off after dark. I reckon the Shoshones are going."

He pointed to the hilltop where the Indians in a compact body were watching the retreat of the night riders. But, despite their war-like front, the women along the ditch bank were packing their bundles to go. The great heat had come, but, much as they feared it, they feared Val Bodie more. For, although Bodie was married to a squaw, his kinsmen were Paiutes with whom the Shoshones were continually at war. And he had a ruthless way with Indians, of shooting first and talking afterward, that had intimidated even Panamint Tom.

"Me stay!" spoke up Captain Jack at Lightfoot's elbow, and Chatfield looked him over appraisingly. With his scouts and retainers gone he would need the Indian's services, but he only glanced dourly at Lightfoot.

"All right, Jack," responded Johnny. "You stay inside this fence and Eatum-Up Jake won't get you. I'll take 'em on any time!"

"By grab!" Chatfield laughed. "You shore think a lot of this Injun, standing up against that bunch the way you did. I don't trust 'em very far myself."

"Me good Injun," stated Jack. "Horse-Ketchum good Hiko man. We friends, eh?" And he held out his hand.

"You bet!" returned Johnny, shaking hands with him indulgently. "And we'll stick together, Jack. Then, bimeby, when it gets hot, if you help me steal my woman, I'll let you go back to your wife."

"Ho! Good!" assented Jack, striding off to un-
pack the mules.

The white men sought the shelter of the house.

Already in the south a solid wall of dust announced the approach of another sandstorm. The
trees were whipping in the wind, and about them,
finer than sand, the storm-borne silt was dropping.
It touched the sweaty hands of people and set in
tiny cakes that formed gray spots of cement, and
all the time, as the wind howled louder, the size of
the gravel grew. But behind their stout stockade
they escaped its full force, and the corridor between the houses was cool.

All that night, watch after watch, the two white
men took turns standing guard, but Val Bodie and
his men did not come. Lightfoot rose at dawn and
looked out over a sand-strewn world, so desolate
and empty that they seemed like human atoms, set
down in a bottomless void. Yet up on the sharp-
topped butte where the Shoshones had kept their
camp a man sat, sphinx-like, his gun across his
knees, his back humped against the wind.

"It's Riley Sloper," pronounced Chatfield. "The
deathwatch is set. But I don't want to kill him. He's
a Tolliver."

"Well, maybe," hinted Lightfoot, "I can take him
off your hands. You know what I said . . . to little
Jim."

"Little Jim is a Tolliver, too," responded Chatfield slowly. "No, Johnny, let's wait for the heat."

The blazing sun topped the Funeral Range, and
no wind came sweeping in to mitigate its sullen
intensity. By ten in the morning, the salt marshes
had begun to steam, and the death-watcher left his

butte. A black haze rose up from the miles of slimy sink, where the poisonous brine stewed and smoked, and there came to their nostrils the rank odor of that hell's brew that had snuffed out so many lives.

The cattle gathered along the ditches, half immersed in the running water; the chickens sneaked into the house, and there, before the fan, dogs and humans alike stretched out to endure the heat. It came up from the marshes in panting waves, like the breath of some monster of the deep, as if the crater that once yawned there had opened its vents again, giving off its poison vapors in gasps. All the world seemed a furnace, an oven where men were baked.

Little Jim fretted and wailed.

"Poor little boy," murmured his mother again and again as she held him before the whirling wheel, and, as the cool water splashed over him, a wry smile twisted his face that was mottled with the blistering heat. The hot weather had come, and a huge hand seemed to cover them, crushing them down with malignant hate. As the men paced about, keeping watch for their enemies, they wore towels about their necks to wipe off the blinding sweat that ran down into their eyes. Yet when the sun, like a ball of fire, set behind the towering Panamints, a gaunt form again showed itself on the butte. It was Riley Sloper, and in the madness of the heat Jim Chatfield reached for his gun.

"No!" He cursed as his wife clutched his hand. "It's him or me . . . that's the code."

"Oh, but wait, Jim, wait!" she pleaded. "Think of little Jim . . . and me. Don't shoot. God will strike him with His heat."

"But it's hell," complained Chatfield, "in the bottom of this sink. God never intended a white man to live here. If I kill Sloper, we can go up on the peaks!"

He waved one hand petulantly toward the high summits of the Panamints, where the pine trees stood out against the sky. But she dissuaded him from his purpose. If there was one thing she knew, it was that she didn't want any killing.

As the night came on, they chained the high door of the gate. In the blank darkness of the desert night Jim took up his weary march, ready to fight in defense of his life, but each morning with the dawn the haunting figure came back, to look down from the butte.

"I'll kill him!" swore Chatfield, but each time he held his hand and God sent a greater heat. Puffy clouds rose up like burnished cones of fire and hung motionlessly above the high peaks. They rode up against the wind and turned black at the base. Then a long spout reached down and the cloudburst broke with a thunder that shattered the air. The water poured out in long black feelers that spread to a solid column. It rained, and down some cañon a wall of brushwood came, spewed out by the glut behind, then trees and yellow water and boulders that ground and tumbled until they rolled far out on the flat. The flood spent its force with magical quickness, and, as the last rush cleared the cañon, its front swept down into the sink.

Before a pageantry like this the people lived on day by day as the rainy season reached its height, but not a drop came to cool their fevered lips for the bottom of the valley was dry. Nor did the thirsty mountains feel the wash of driving rains.

Some cañon, parched before, was inundated by a flood—the rest of the desert remained dry. They endured, since they must, and every day at dawn Riley Sloper stood out on his butte.

Never once in a month of waiting had he ventured near the ranch, although they knew what his errand was. He seemed in his crack-brained way to be courting the very death that Dad Tolliver had sent him to deal. An ambush at dawn, a bullet from the brush as he stepped out against the sky, and this clean-strain killer of the Tolliver clan would be wiped out by a shot. Yet, crazed as Chatfield was, his wife persuaded him not to do it, and the deathwatch continued. Val Bodie and his men had long since left, and one evening Lightfoot saddled Paynim.

By the banks of the rushing ditch, tied, as it were, to a haystack, the golden stallion had fretted impatiently—and always he looked to the north. Now, as he felt his master's hand and champed the familiar bit, he snuffed the heated wind and whickered. He knew without words that their ride would take him home, to the cañon where his mates frisked and played.

"Be quiet," admonished Lightfoot, laying a hand on his nose as he passed him out the tall gate, and Paynim snorted softly. Then, as Lightfoot swung up, he ambled off through the night, at last breaking into a lope. Cow Springs lay behind them, and ahead were Moonbeam—and Diana.

Chapter Twenty-three

A blanket of clouds overhung Devil's Mountain as Johnny Lightfoot rode north through the night, and above Enúpi Kai the heat lightning stabbed and blinked, brewing a storm for the coming day.

Strange winds came rushing in, whipping the sandhills to a spume that leaped up against the murky sky, but Paynim kept on, ever tugging at the bit, never tiring, although the heat brought the sweat. As he loped on, he whickered softly.

All his life had been spent in this Valley of Death, where only the strongest could survive. He was desert-bred, and his sires before him had known nothing but sand and heat. Lightfoot dropped the reins and gave him his head, and on the shore of the dry lake Paynim finally stopped. There was a shimmer in the starlight—water lapped at his feet. The dry lake had come back to its own, and the clouds above the peaks rumbled forbiddingly.

The stallion turned away, fighting his head to circle the lake, trotting anxiously until he found the familiar wash. At the entrance to the gateway, where the rock dam blocked their path, he snorted and came to a halt. Then he neighed, loud and shrill, his heart wild with longing. But no mate answered his call.

He neighed louder, in frenzied appeal, dropping his nose to the ground in a long, sobbing grunt of despair. Now at last he knew the reason why his master had not turned homeward. Paynim turned back toward Toógahboth.

The dawn found them safely hidden among the ancient mesquites whose roots, while their tops were bathed in fire, drank deeply of the flood water at their feet. There was no water hole now to tempt the wild mustangs to their fate. All the broad, silvery flat where the moon horses had gamboled was covered by an inch-deep sea. Every day some barren cañon belched out its charge of waters to fill up the shallow lake further, but quickly as it came, the sun drank it up, while the clouds poured down more rain.

As the sun swung up, like a flaming shield before the face of an angry god, Lightfoot saw the thunderheads rise, higher and higher above the mountains until they puffed out in fluffy white cones. They turned black at the base and between two monstrous clouds the lightning stabbed back and forth threateningly. Then they moved together, slowly, while the cañons reëchoed to the rumble of their thunderous booming. The mighty forces of Nature seemed set in battle array, cloud bearing down on cloud while the storm gods who rode their crests smote the earth with bolts of fire.

Beneath them, stunned and awed by the majesty of the combat, Lightfoot watched the cohorts of the sky as they wheeled above the mountain peaks. What if, among those cañons, the gods should descend upon where Diana was and scour out the dam at its gateway? With what joy would he ride up the newly made road and bring her the news of her freedom. But the clouds swung away, farther and farther to the north, retiring sullenly with muttered detonations.

A sense of loss and disappointment, of thwarted hope and unreasoning fear, drove Lightfoot to the shelter of the trees. How could he, a mere atom in the cosmos, hope to turn the forces of Nature to do his will? And yet he watched, for a man can hope. Every day the storm struck somewhere—some cañon was swept bare. And how could Devil's Cañon escape, when others on both sides had caught the sluicing descent of the cloudbursts?

There was a *crash* along the peaks, a thunderous reverberation that announced that the storm gods had struck, and, as Lightfoot leaped up, he felt the earth tremble beneath him with the shock of another, mightier stroke. Then with a smashing *clap* of thunder the two clouds rushed together and their base turned black as ink.

The bottom broke and a snaky waterspout reached down toward the jagged peaks, whipping back and forth—seeking the spot. Where it fell, the waste of ages would be swept clean away, leaving the bedrock white and bare. Johnny found himself praying, trying to move with his puny hands this avalanche of water across the sky. But it drifted off to the north, and, as the solid column fell, he could see that Devil's Cañon had escaped.

The cloud opened, like a bag from which the bottom is ripped, and the rain poured, inky black, through the hole. As if drawn in by the suction, the thunderhead floated above it, sagging lower till the peaks were obscured. Lightfoot waited expectantly, his eyes on the cañons to the north, until at last a leaping mass belched out of its narrow throat and swept down toward the lake. Another followed, and he saw the impetuous rush of the torrent as it battled its way out through the passage.

Then from Devil's Cañon itself a mountain of rocks shot forth with a roar that stopped his heart.

The spout had shifted, behind its curtain of mist, touching the headwaters of three cañons as it fell, and the barrier across the gateway had gone down. A deluge of yellow foam overlapped it and swept on, carrying tree trunks on its crest like straws, and through his glasses Lightfoot could see the churning waves of the torrent as they bore the shattered boulders along.

There was no room before its front for anything that could move, and it swept the gateway clean with a rush. The forefront of the water moved forward like a wall, spreading out as the sand washes diverted it, and before the first wave had lapped into the turbid lake the glut at the gateway had passed. The resistless hand of Nature had performed within an hour the work of 1,000 men.

Lightfoot was astounded by the swiftness of this hand that had opened the way before him. He felt as if in some way he had broken the dam himself, by the force of his muttered prayer. He felt great, exalted, the particular god of all that land where nobody dwelt but him. But as the waters spent their strength and the washes ran quickly dry, he shook off the spell that had held him in its thrall and threw the saddle on Paynim.

Devil's Cañon was open, and he circled the muddy lake till he stood on the bank of the wash. The level sand was firm—it had set like cement—and Paynim stepped out on it confidently. Then, fighting his head, he trotted off up the wash until he stood before the shattered gateway. The great wall that had towered there had been swept clean away, filling up the deep pool of the waterfall.

Their way had been made straight by the hand of God, and Paynim raised his golden head and neighed.

Up over the battered wall he scrambled on the jump, splashing madly through the water as they forded the muddy creek, which was running knee-deep among the rocks. All about them lay the wreckage of the trees and fields above, the stranded trunks of cottonwoods, scattered remnants of the fence, an ore pan from Morgan's mine.

Lightfoot had a vision of the cañon as it had been before the cloudburst had worked its will. The same hand that had opened the gateway might have destroyed all behind it—the golden horses, the mine, Diana. But who could doubt a God who had given so much? Lightfoot pressed on, and the cave appeared before him.

The wave of mud from the first rush of the flood had been halted almost at its door where the cow-hide still hung by its thongs, and the trees along the cañon wall stood firmly. But down the middle of the creekbed a huge trench had been sluiced—trees, garden, fence, and all were gone. The surging waters had overwhelmed them, half burying them in débris, and then the run-off had cut a deep ditch. Johnny reined over toward the cave, over-come by gloomy thoughts, starting nervously at every sound.

The cañon was empty now and only the bab-bling creek woke the echoes of the penthouse walls. But upon the cliff, not a month before, he had seen a golden head—and one of Diana's foxes, making off. He had seen her father, too, waving his rifle like a madman as he poised on the edge of the abyss. What if he was lurking now, waiting to wreak a belated revenge? What if Diana has been lost in the flood?

Lightfoot halted before the doorway, too unstrung to venture in, and listened. Then Paynim pricked up his ears, whirled, raised his head, and loudly and shrilly against the wind gave the call to his mates.

There was a silence, while the water babbled louder over its rocks, and the cliffs echoed back the neigh, but Paynim had heard what his master could not hear and he started at a trot up the creek.

Johnny saw a track before him, sunk deep in the half-dried mud, the imprint of huge moccasins, leading the way in long strides—the footprints of Frying-Pan George. Yet he did not draw rein for, across the ravaged creekbed, the wooded pasture lay unspoiled. Tossing heads rose and fell among the clustering mesquite trees, where a herd of horses came running. Then, out from the thorny thicket, Diana came at a gallop, and behind her the nine golden steeds.

She stopped short at sight of Paynim—and a strange man in her cañon where before only her father had dwelt—but when Johnny raised his hand, she swung low on Moonbeam's neck and came plunging up the cutbank of the creek. Her hair was flying wildly. She was splashed with sand and mud, but her eyes glowed like stars when she met him face to face and dropped down, trembling, from her horse.

"Oh, Johnny!" she cried, throwing her arms about his neck. "I'm so glad!" And she gave him a hug. "Oh, Johnny," she breathed again and kissed him on both cheeks. "I never looked to see you again."

"Here, too," responded Lightfoot, returning the hug and kisses gaily. "I was down there at Night Water when the cloudburst opened the gateway. And believe me, I rode right up."

"Up the cañon? Is it open? Oh, then, Johnny, we must run, because if Father comes back, he'll kill you."

"I reckon he will," assented Lightfoot. "Let's be riding right now. There's his tracks, going up to the mine."

"He's crazy," she whispered. "The storm washed off half his ore that he'd piled up by the dump. I was afraid to go near him, he cursed and shouted so. Oh, Johnny, I'm glad you've come."

She buried her face against his breast, and he patted her soothingly while his eyes searched the country above. The cloudburst had come down the narrow cañon to the north where Morgan had driven his tunnel. Then, taking a sharp turn, it had piled up a mountain of débris and swept on down the creek. Rocks and boulders were strewn everywhere, cemented fast in mud, and somewhere in that chaos Randolph Morgan was searching for his gold.

"Let's go, right now," spoke up Johnny. He kissed her as he turned to mount.

She was pale and frightened, and yet her eyes as she looked back at him were big and tender with love.

"Yes, Johnny," she answered, and scrambled up on Moonbeam, who was standing nose to nose with Paynim. Then with a kick of the heel she dashed ahead toward the cave, dropping off to dart in through the door.

Lightfoot followed fast, one eye on the trail behind, the other on the cowhide door.

"Come on!" he called. "Don't stop for your clothes! My God, don't take so long!"

A frenzy of impatience came over him as he waited, but Diana lingered on.

"I'm getting mother's jewels!" she replied in muffled tones. "But he seems to have hidden them somewhere!"

"Let 'em go!" he yelled. "Do you want me to get killed?" And from far up the cañon there came a series of shouts.

"Come out of there!" he cried, dropping down off his horse to rush inside the door.

"I've found them!" she responded, running out of an inner chamber. "But Johnny, I can't find Christopher!"

"Christopher who?" he demanded, catching her up in his arms and carrying her out the door. "Can't you hear? Your father is coming!"

"Yes, but Christopher!" she sobbed. "My dear little fox, you know! And, oh, now Columbus is gone!"

"Let 'em go," entreated Lightfoot, "and pile up on that horse!"

As he spoke a savage shouting rent the air. It was Morgan, cursing the storm as he strode back from his mine. But he had not rounded the turn. Lightfoot caught the glint of a rifle in his hands as he came around the point, and snatched Diana in a panic.

"Ride!" he yelled. "Or I'll be killed sure as hell!" And he swung her up on her horse. Paynim reared and flew back, but Johnny mounted on the fly, and they were off in a shower of mud. Hanging low on Paynim's neck, Lightfoot listened for the bullets, but the old man did not shoot. He was running like a madman to catch a horse from the remuda. But as he ran, he held fast to his gun.

"He's coming!" warned Johnny, and took the lead like a shot. It was Paynim, the sire, against his son—the stallion against his own flesh and blood.

Chapter Twenty-four

The sun gleamed like fire on the flooded floor of the lake as Lightfoot raced out of Devil's Cañon, and the steam of drying mud along the course of the cloudburst made Lost Valley smoke like a caldron.

No wind stirred the sultry air, and, even while they rode, Lightfoot felt the blinding stroke of the heat. Yet the devil man was behind them, and, although death lay ahead, Johnny spurred on into the abyss.

Around the shore of the shallow lagoon they rode side-by-side, Diana still clutching the casket of jewels that had tempted her to dally too long. She knew now that, for her heirlooms, she might lose her lover, or compel him to kill her father. Yet even as she fled, looking back up the long wash, she remembered her precious pet foxes. It was for them more than the jewels that she had searched the darkened cave, and she murmured their names regretfully.

"Never mind about Christopher," answered Lightfoot shortly. "We've got to ride these horses down to get away from your father. They can't go far in this heat."

"Oh, there he comes now!" cried Diana. "On Turco!"

A flash of gold at the cañon mouth turned into a thoroughbred racer, driven on at a furious pace by the old man on its back, who waved his rifle as he spied them. Johnny had circled the lake, but Morgan charged into it impetuously, cutting across on a tangent to bring him within rifle shot, reckoning nothing of the perils ahead. Almost before they knew it, he had made up half the distance, but in the middle of the lake, where the bottom was soft, Turco labored and almost stopped.

"Come on!" yelled Lightfoot as Diana looked back fearfully. "He's stuck! He'll have to turn back! Let him shoot if he wants to! We'll keep up ahead of him and lose him in the sandhills tonight!"

Morgan urged his racer on, deeper and deeper into the slough, but the more Turco floundered, the more he became bogged until at last he came to a halt. The madman on his back had driven him so far, but Turco knew the mud holes ahead. Since he had been a colt he had waded in the lake, when the cloudbursts flooded the *playa* with mud, but where the water had stood longest no horse or man could cross, and he turned stubbornly back toward the shore. Morgan fought him in a fury, and, when he finally won the farther shore, Lightfoot and Diana were gone.

Down the Death Valley trail, past the ever-drifting sandhills that radiated a suffocating heat, they fled on regardless of the precious animals they rode—horses worth almost their weight in gold. The blood of kings coursed in their veins, but now they felt the whip, and so they galloped till the night closed down. They had escaped, although behind them Morgan was spurring on their trail. Darkness would hide them now.

Lightfoot turned out of the burro path that led on to Esahbwoó, where the emigrants had perished long before, and dismounted to breathe his mount. Noble-hearted Paynim, his shoulders flecked with foam, spread his forehoofs and bowed like a grampus. The race had sapped his strength, after the long ride the night before and his day in the sweltering heat, but after his master had rubbed him down and patted his neck, he turned and followed Moonbeam south. He had won her again, the queen of his *manada*, but a heat had come upon them that almost stopped their breath and he took the trail at a walk.

Never before in his long stay at Furnace Creek had Johnny Lightfoot known such a night. Even after the sun had set, the ground gave off heat, as if the crater far beneath them had come to life. The earth seemed to sweat out a poisonous gas—the rank smell of decaying marshes, cooking and stewing like a hell broth—and the air moved in hot, blasting gasps. After daring storm and flood to rescue Diana from her cañon, he had brought her into the stark presence of death.

Always before, as the night wore on, the air had become cooler, but now the heat seemed to increase. To save their spent horses they dismounted and walked, stopping often to listen for pursuit, and in the silence of the desert Johnny told her of her cousins, and of the welcome that awaited them at the ranch.

It appeared before them at dawn, like a mirage in the distance, and Paynim pricked up his ears. The tall palms brought up visions of running water and shady nooks, and Moonbeam whickered joyously.

"Another mile and we're there," said Lightfoot, mounting.

Diana swung in beside him. Her face was pale and bloodless from the exhaustion that comes from heat, but, as they trotted toward the ranch, she smiled.

"Isn't it beautiful?" She sighed. "Is that Cousin Jim at the gate? But who is that other man? He's running!"

She pointed to the butte down which a scarecrow figure was coming, and Lightfoot jumped Paynim into a gallop.

"Come on!" he yelled. "That's Riley Sloper! He's a Tolliver! Been trying to kill Jim for a month!"

He looked back toward the butte, where day after day the feudist had kept his deathwatch, but now Sloper was shambling toward him at a crazy, high-stepping lope.

"He's locoed with the heat!" cried Lightfoot in dismay as Riley stopped and whipped up his rifle. As if they sensed their danger, the two horses raced away, while their riders swung low along their necks. Sloper had halted on a knoll, his neck craned, his rifle extended as he followed the course of their race, but as he drew a bead on Johnny, there was a shot from the gate. He jumped and dropped his rifle. Jim Chatfield had been watching him, and now, after months of jockeying, the rival clansmen were at last shooting it out.

Sloper ducked behind a bush and made a run to get his rifle, but with the sureness of death itself Chatfield's rifle spoke again and his enemy went down, sprawling. A puff of dust had risen before him. There was a commotion behind the brush, and then, left-handed, Riley Sloper drew his pistol and shot back at the man he aimed to kill. But when, deliberately, Jim raised his rifle to shoot, Sloper ran like a wounded buck.

"I winged him!" shouted Chatfield as Lightfoot rode up to the gate. "Take her in to Damaris! Sloper'll be back!"

He stepped aside to let them pass, his keen eyes following Sloper's flight, and that was Diana's welcome to Furnace Creek.

But once inside the gateway, Damaris came running and greeted her with a kiss.

"Are you Diana?" she cried. "Diana Morgan? Then come right in, dear, out of the heat!"

Johnny gazed after them dumbly as they passed in, arm and arm, to seek the cool darkness of the house. As Captain Jack hurried out to take charge of the horses, he staggered in and wet his throbbing head. Although the sun had hardly risen, it was like the heat of midday, and he stretched out with a sigh before the fan. Without the splash of its water, the busy swirl of its sturdy wings, how else could a man hope to endure the day to come, and the inferno of another night? He closed his bloodshot eyes and breathed deeply as his muscles relaxed—then he passed into a dreamless sleep.

For two nights and a day, without sleep or rest, he had ridden on his quest, and now, safely home, he left Diana to her kinsfolk, and Jim to guard the gate.

The *crack* of a rifle roused Lightfoot, and Captain Jack rushed in, seeking shelter from the fray.

"Devil man . . . she come!" he gasped, rolling his eyes. "Devil man from Enúpi Kai! Riley Sloper run shootum . . . Jim Chatfield shootum. Fightum now . . . devil man fall down!"

"Hell's bells!" exclaimed Lightfoot as he looked about for his guns. "The old man is on the warpath!"

But when he ran out to the gate, Randolph Morgan was on the ground and his horse was standing over him.

"They've gone crazy, both of them!" cursed Chatfield, his eyes gleaming wickedly. "Riley Sloper went hog wild and came down to kill him, and the old man rode out to meet him. They were shooting it out when I ran Riley off. Do you reckon that's my uncle Randolph?"

"I know it," answered Lightfoot. "And he was crazy before he started. Came down here on purpose to kill me, so I'm glad he tangled with Riley. By grab, Jim, this is getting dangerous."

"Well, let's go out and bring him in," responded Chatfield shortly, "before he perishes in the sun. And then Riley Sloper can play hell, if he wants to. I'm going to get back to that fan."

He started down the road, still watching the brush for the hobgoblin form of Sloper, but the feudist had fled up the bank of the ditch, and they hurried on to Morgan.

He lay piled up among the rocks. His horse in flying back had dumped him on his head. In one outstretched hand he still clutched the pistol with which he had been firing when he fell. Lightfoot looked him over grimly, kicked aside the hot gun, and helped lay him across the back of his horse. Except for the accident of the chance encounter with Riley Sloper, the old man's gun would have been turned on Lightfoot. But now Morgan was stunned by his fall among the boulders.

They bore him back to the house.

"He's crazy ... we're all crazy," croaked Chatfield, as they laid Morgan in front of the fan. "The man don't live that can stand out in that sun and not have his brains begin to cook. Take care of him while I soak my haid!" And he plunged his head into the ditch.

Johnny followed him, for the exertion in the broiling sun had made his senses reel. He was dizzy, and the throb of blood in his brain was like a hammer stroke against his skull. The world seemed obscured, and, as he lay gasping before the fan, he dreamed crazily of fighting and sudden death. Riley Sloper—Randolph Morgan—they met and merged before his eyes into a creature of inconceivable hate, and then the saturnine visage of Jim Chatfield appeared, his keen eyes gleaming murderously. They were all out to kill—the heat had overthrown their reason. But the fan was bringing it back.

Lightfoot felt the splash of water against his face—warm water, almost hot, but turning cool in an instant before the breeze stirred up by the fan. How had anyone lived in that inferno of heat before the fan had been set in place? The same water that turned the millwheel splashed the ground and the people on it, people who sprawled on the wet earth as abjectly as animals, asked nothing but to drink, and drink again. In that furnace-like atmosphere a pint of water was nothing. They drank gallons of it in a day and from every pore at once the blinding sweat poured out.

Lightfoot glanced up at the women who sat close to the fan, with little Jim lying between them. The child was stark naked. His face was as mottled as a newborn babe's, but his little body was cool. Randolph Morgan lay next, his white beard whipping in the breeze, his eyes closed as if in death. But his breast rose rhythmically, and Johnny knew he was alive. And, with him, to be alive was to be dangerous. Jim Chatfield sat close to Lightfoot, his back against the wall, his lantern jaw grimly set. He alone watched the gateway, and at his side laid the rifle that had sent so many Tollivers to their reward.

Lightfoot dozed off, wondering vaguely at the fate that had led him to such a place. Not a day's journey away the Shoshones were looking down on them from high mountains, covered with pines. But they, the superior white people, lay frying in their fat to feed some ancient grudge. It was the feud that had driven them, every one, to this inferno—Jim Chatfield, Riley Sloper, Randolph Morgan. And what a breed of fighters they were. So dangerous and yet so loyal, willing to lay down their lives for their clan. Even the heat had not driven them to a truce.

Behind them all, his stolid face beaded with sweat, sat the Indian, Captain Jack. He was stripped to the waist, his sturdy feet were bare, and at sight of Lightfoot he grinned. This valley was his home, the ancient dwelling place of his people, and patiently he endured the torment. But as he sat there, he, too, watched the gate. Somewhere out in the hills, wounded and crazed by the heat, Riley Sloper roamed at large, as dangerous as a sidewinder, ready to strike at the first thing that moved.

A black haze, like a pall of smoke, obscured the sun as the marshes boiled, filling the air with a sweltering humidity, and in a darkness like that of an eclipse the sufferers fell silent, as if the end of the world were at hand. Such a heat as they endured had never been felt before—the thermometer stood at 134°—and men, dogs, and chickens, even the wood rats from the mesquite pile, laid themselves out in the track of the fan. But suddenly, when the fever in their blood was at its highest, the splashing of the water wheel ceased.

Jim Chatfield rose up, muttering fretfully under his breath as he hurried to look at the flume. Then his voice rang out sharply in a staccato of angry curses, and Damaris started up anxiously.

"What's the matter, dear?" she called, and his answer was like a death sentence.

"The ditch is dry!" he yelled. "Riley Sloper has cut it! Ketch some water or we won't have a drop!"

Chapter Twenty-five

There is a madness that comes from heat, making the wanderer on the desert run in circles and dig holes in the sand. It drives prospectors to kill their partners for a canteen of water, and the only escape is to rest. Lying still in the shade, although the blood pounds like mad and the senses reel from the sun, the slender thread of reason holds men back from a race to their death. But once they begin to run they are lost.

Before the cool draft of their fan the heat-sick people at Furnace Creek had escaped the ultimate madness that brings death, but with the water wheel stilled they leaped up one by one in a fever of distracted fear. Damaris clutched her baby, trying to still its feeble wails. Jim Chatfield reached for his gun. But when he started up the ditch, muttering threats against Riley Sloper, his wife caught him by the arm.

"Jim," she said, "if you go, it will kill you. No man can live in that sun."

"Riley Sloper lived!" he yapped. "He lived to cut my ditch. I believe he waited on purpose."

"No, no, Jim, dear," she reasoned. "Riley is out of his head. We can stand it until night, and then you can go up there. But if you go now, it will mean your death."

"I'm going to kill Riley Sloper if it's my last act!" raved Chatfield. "This is murder . . . killing women and children! And who's going to mend the ditch, unless I do it?" he demanded.

"I will," spoke up Johnny Lightfoot. But as he reached for a shovel, Captain Jack pushed him gently aside.

"Me go!" he said. "You lay down . . . keep still. Pretty soon you hear water come back."

"All right, Jack." Johnny smiled. "I believe you can stand it. But if one of us Hiko men goes out in that sun and. . . ."

"No good . . . killum dead." The Indian nodded, and with an answering smile he was gone.

They lay down in the sweltering corridor, where the hot dampness from the wet ground seemed almost to stop their breath, and so the long ordeal began. But one by one they rose up and went outside, for their veins seemed running with fire. There was no water left to drink, and a hot wind from the sink made their lips dry up and crack. The leaves on the lush cottonwoods hung, curled-up and drooping, and, as the swallows from under the leaves felt the mad urge to fly, they dropped dead as they circled the fields. The world was burning up, and they were burning with it, without even the chance of a drink of water.

In tense silence or cursing brokenly Jim Chatfield paced the porch, looking off up the ditch for Captain Jack. But the Indian had disappeared, creeping slowly up the streambed to gain the scant shade of the mesquites.

"I'm going," repeated Chatfield, over and over like a litany. But Damaris shook her head. Little Jim had begun to wail with thin, choking cries that stabbed at his mother's heart, but she sat beside him, fanning, while Diana on the other side put the last drop of water to his lips. Lightfoot had waited, but now, as he met her eyes, he beckoned Jim Chatfield aside.

"You stay here," he said. "I'm going up the ditch."

Chatfield nodded glumly.

"All right," he answered. "Damn an Injun, anyway. Much obliged, Johnny . . . it's my turn next."

He paced away, but as Lightfoot started up the ditch, he heard the *gurgle* of water at his feet. It came rushing, as if eager to run down the flume and dash against the paddles of the wheel, and Lightfoot whooped as it passed.

"Here it comes!" he yelled. "Here's the water! Water!" And the great wheel groaned on its gudgeons. Then with a splash from its paddles it sent the broad wings spinning, and everyone came running. They were laughing like children as they drank deeply and wet their heads and laid the baby out on damp sacks, but as they settled down to rest, Lightfoot remembered the Indian, for Captain Jack had not come back.

"Oh, he's all right," reasoned Jim. "They's no use going up there. I'd just have to go out after you." And so they waited until the sun sank behind the Panamints and the terrible day was done.

But when evening approached and Captain Jack did not come, Lightfoot started off up the ditch.

"Wait a minute," called Chatfield, "and I'll go along with you! He may have had trouble with Riley!"

He wrapped a rag around his rifle and hung it through his arm, for the metal was blistering hot, and, as they moved up toward the hills, Johnny saw his keen eyes searching out every tree and bush.

"If I find that Riley Sloper," he said at last, "I'll shoot him like a dog. A man is a fool to listen to his womenfolks ... I should have killed him long ago."

"I believe you're right." Lightfoot nodded. "I couldn't savvy what he was waiting for. . . ."

"The murdering whelp was, waiting to kill my wife ... and my baby that's half a Tolliver. But he knowed his only chance ... and not get hung for it ... was to ketch us in a big spell of heat. A man like that don't deserve no pity. I'll kill him like a broken-back rattlesnake!"

Chatfield strode ahead, muttering, but as he approached the mouth of the cañon, Captain Jack rose up and pointed. Then he held up a rifle and a pair of six-shooters and the white men understood. Crawling and groveling down a dry wash, his clothes torn from his back and his matted hair covering his face, Riley Sloper, stark mad, was whimpering like a fox as he dug furtive holes in the sand. Jim Chatfield watched him coldly, then glanced at the break where Captain Jack had mended the ditch.

"Did he do that?" he asked.

Jack nodded. "She crazy." He grinned. "All time diggum hole. All time cry ... say killum little boy."

"Yes, damn his cowardly heart!" gritted Chatfield. "I knowed he done it on purpose. Cut that ditch, by grab, jest like he'd cut a man's throat. He knowed it would kill my boy."

He raised his rifle slowly, then dropped it to his side, and slouched off farther up the gulch.

Riley Sloper was digging away against the cutbank of the wash, and, when they came, he did not stop or look up. His right hand was torn and bloody, where Chatfield's bullet had shattered it; his naked back was burned by the sun, but he dug on, talking to himself.

"Pore leetle feller . . . and a Tolliver, too. But Dad told me I had to kill Jim. He's a Chatfield, damn his heart . . . and he went and stole Damaris. Stole a Tolliver . . . and crossed the blood."

"Well, what of it, you danged skunk?" demanded Chatfield roughly, giving him a jab in the ribs with his gun. "Look up here and quit your diggin' . . . and say your prayers, if you know any, because I'm going to blow your haid off!"

Sloper fell over sidewise and stared up with vacant eyes, then returned to his ceaseless digging.

"Water!" he croaked. "I've got to find water. That sun is killing me! But I cain't go away . . . I've got to kill Jim first. He's a Chatfield and he done stole Damaris."

"He's crazy!" pronounced Chatfield. "Take him and throw him in the ditch. I hate to shoot him. But you heard what he said . . . I've got my wife and baby to think of."

"Let's take him down to the house," proposed Lightfoot as they watched Sloper drink at the ditch. "He was crazy when I came at sunup this morning. What will the womenfolks say if you kill him?"

"Yes, that's it," grumbled Jim. "I should've shot him on sight. Now Damaris will know . . . and, of course, he's a Tolliver. Well, tote him along, then . . . he's gaunted down to a shadder. But they's no good will come from it. He's a killer."

They bore him back down the gulch, the mere skeleton of a man, and laid him down in front of the fan. After Damaris had gazed fearfully at his stern and wasted countenance, she turned and smiled at her husband.

"I knew you wouldn't kill him," she said. "Oh, Jim!" And she kissed his cheek.

Chapter Twenty-six

The terrible night came on and they lay sprawling in front of the fan, but toward midnight a great roaring aroused them, and the angry whoop of the wind. Then a sandstorm swept in, blowing away the humid vapors that had risen from the marshy sink, and one by one the sufferers slept. In front of the fan little Jim's chubby fists relaxed and his feeble wail died away. His mother stretched out beside him—as did Diana, tired and frightened, who had fled in vain from her fate, Now her father, tossing and muttering, lay side-by-side with Riley Sloper, and both talked of killing as they slept. The old man, bent with years, and the austere and hardy feudist—and, as she listened, Diana wept. Her father had told the truth—all men were beasts and murderers. Even Johnny avoided her now. And the world she had dreamed of beyond the walls of her cañon—was this the land of her dreams? What heat, what madness, what tragedy lay all about her! And on the morrow—what would happen then? She crept closer to Damaris and put one hand in hers, and so fell asleep.

Outside, the rush and rattle of the windstorm had ceased, and a coolness drew down into the Valley of Death that soothed the weary sleepers by the fan. Chatfield rose with the dawn and stood gazing at Riley Sloper, and the old man who huddled by his side. Then Jim took all the guns except his own and Lightfoot's and locked them up in his room. Death had come close enough during the madness of the heat. He beckoned, and Lightfoot followed him out.

"Watch Riley," Chatfield warned. "I'll take care of Uncle Randolph. I don't reckon he'll kill you now."

"He thinks I stole his daughter," explained Johnny. "You tell him I brought her straight to you."

"I see." Chatfield nodded. "Well, I happened to know you, Johnny, and I'll tell him you're a damned good man. A good man . . . and I'll never forget your starting off up that gulch. Let's go out and look after the stock."

They paced out wearily, like men old before their time, and on the bare ground before them they saw the bodies of swallows, struck dead as they flew through the heat. Under the fronds of the palms, hawks and owls stared out, stupefied, still hiding from the long-vanished sun. But beneath the cottonwoods that stood along the ditch they found their horses, feeding. Paynim and Moonbeam looked up at Johnny and whickered—the heat had not even thinned their blood. But High Behind stood drooping, and at sight of his master he whinnied forth a frenzied appeal.

"He wants me to take him out of here," observed Lightfoot grimly. "And I believe, by the gods, he's right."

"The heat's over," Chatfield assured him earnestly. "But we were lucky to come through it alive. If it wasn't for Riley Sloper, I'd leave here tomorrow. Stay around until we see which way he jumps."

"I'll stay," promised Johnny, "but you keep your eye on Morgan. I don't dare speak to Diana."

"You'd better not," advised Jim, "until I get a chance to talk to him. But Riley is dangerous . . . he's a killer."

They threw down hay for their horses and started a fire in the kitchen stove, and at the fragrance of boiling coffee all the sleepers arose, except Riley Sloper and Morgan. Sloper opened his eyes and stared up dully as he heard the women bustling about, but only when Damaris brought him a cup of hot coffee did he rouse up and look around.

"Where am I, ma'am?" he asked. "I seem to be sick . . . but I recollect seeing you, somewhar."

"You're with friends," she answered sweetly. "I'll take care of you, Mister Sloper. Now take a good drink and you'll be stronger."

He clutched the cup feebly and drained it to the bottom, and then he looked her over again.

"Why, you're Damaris!" he exclaimed. "I knowed I'd seen you somewhar. But what's the matter with my hand?"

He held up his bandaged arm and she saw his mind was wandering—he had forgotten where he was.

"You've been fighting," she said reproachfully. "And somebody shot you. But Jim wrapped it and. . . ."

"Jim?" he repeated. "Jim who?"

"Why, my husband!" she cried. "Didn't you know I was married? Jim Chatfield . . . and this is our baby."

She held up little Jim who had already been cared for. The feudist regarded her strangely.

"I remember now," he said. "I used to see him through my telescope . . . and you holding him, thar by the door. But did Jim Chatfield fix my hand?"

"Yes, and he went out and got you when you were crazy with the heat. You don't want to fight him now, do you?"

"Not me," answered Sloper. "I've got enough of fighting. And Jim Chatfield helped me . . . a Tolliver."

"Yes, Riley, he helped you," she went on earnestly, "because Jim and I are married now. He promised me he'd never fight the Tollivers again, except to protect his life."

"He hit me," spoke up Sloper, "but I don't reckon he meant to kill me. Because back home Jim was always a dead shot."

"He is now," said Damaris, "but Jim likes you, Riley. Won't you please shake hands and be friends?"

She bent over him pleadingly, but his stern eyes flashed fire.

"I don't shake hands with no Chatfield!" he declared.

"Well, shake hands with little Jim, then," she urged. "He's a Tolliver . . . James Tolliver Chatfield." And she thrust out a tiny hand.

"I don't care if I do," stated Sloper judicially, and he took the little hand in his own. Then for a long time he sat staring at the mother and child, and at last he beckoned her nearer.

"I'll shake hands with Jim," he said

She called to her husband. "Jim," she beamed, "Riley has shook hands with baby, and now he'll shake hands with you!"

"No, he won't!" burst out Chatfield, coming closer. His anger seemed to have the better of him. "Damn your black heart, Riley. You tried to kill my wife and child."

"I know it . . . I admit it," responded Sloper tremulously. "But, Jim, I'm sorry I done it. Her own father told me to do it."

"My father!" she cried incredulously.

"Yes, ma'am, your own father, Dad Tolliver. But I reckon now he was out of his haid. He told me to find you, no matter whar you hid. It was a grievous thing to do, but I done it. But I don't reckon he knowed about little Jim hyar . . . and the blood being crossed and all. The feud don't hold now . . . and I'm going to ask you, Jim, to take the hand of a Tolliver."

He held out his wounded hand, and as Chatfield took it grimly, Damaris hugged her baby and wept.

Chapter Twenty-seven

The feud that had cost hundreds of lives—spreading down from the rugged mountains to the bluegrass valleys of Kentucky—was over, like the heat, in a day. Riley Sloper, who had gone through the tortures of hell to wreak vengeance for the insult of his clan, sat meekly in the shade while the man who had shot him applied balsam to his wounded hand. They said little, for old wounds are easily opened, but always, while they worked, Damaris hovered over them, and now her smile had returned.

She went about her tasks singing, as Johnny Lightfoot had heard her when he had sought refuge from Val Bodie and his gang, but now a greater enemy than Bodie was upon him, watching every move he made. Randolph Morgan was the last of the refugees to recover from the effects of the heat, but when he opened his eyes and saw Lightfoot talking with Chatfield, he sat up and stared.

"This is Johnny Lightfoot, Uncle," began Chatfield. "And I'm your nephew, Jim Chatfield."

"So you say," returned the old man, "but I don't know you at all, suh! That's the rascal who stole my daughter!" He pointed a tremulous finger at Lightfoot and felt around for his gun. "Where's my pistol?" he demanded. "Am I a prisoner in this house? Give me back my guns!"

"You don't need no guns," answered Chatfield

shortly. "And before we go any further, I'd like to correct you. Mistuh Lightfoot never stole your daughter."

"Yes, he did," accused Morgan. "And he stole my horse, too! He took Paynim . . . the best stallion in the band."

"Paynim is out in the corral," spoke up Johnny. "He's yours, when you're ready to go."

"Yes, but where's my daughter, suh?" demanded the old man indignantly. "I saw you, you rascal! You took advantage of her innocence to deceive her and lead her astray! I saw you, suh, when you stole her . . . and all her mother's jewels. . . ."

"Why, Father!" cried Diana who had been listening at the doorway. "Johnny never even touched the jewels!"

"But he touched you!" raged Morgan. "I saw him, stealing your kisses. And what is more precious to a father's heart . . . his daughter or the jewels she wears?"

"Now, Uncle," broke in Damaris, "I don't want you to talk that way. Because Diana asked Johnny to take her out of the cañon . . . and he brought her straight to us."

"I don't know you, madam," responded the old man tartly. "But I know my rights, and my duty as a father. . . ."

"Then I'll inform you," interrupted Damaris, "that I'm Jim Chatfield's wife, and cousin by marriage to Diana. She's been placed in my care, and no one, not even her father. . . ."

"Let her speak for herself, then!" thundered Morgan, rising up and leaning shakily against the wall. "Diana, do you recognize my authority? Are you my daughter, or the cousin of this woman?"

"I'm your daughter," replied Diana meekly. "But Damaris is my cousin, too."

She slipped her hand into Damaris's and faced him fearlessly, while the old man's eyes bored her through.

"Answer my question!" he ordered. "Do you recognize my authority, or have you left my home?"

"I have left the cañon," answered Diana firmly. "Mother told me, when I grew up, that I should go . . . and take her jewels with me."

"Oh, she did, eh?" responded her father after a silence. "Well, why didn't you say so in the first place? It seems to me, after all my care, you might at least say good bye and not decamp like a runaway slave."

"Father," cried Diana, "don't you speak to me like that! Don't you dare to call me such names! You don't love me any more . . . and now that mother is gone, I will stay here with Cousin Damaris."

"Very well," agreed Morgan, taken aback by her anger. "I wash my hands of the whole matter. And now, if you will kindly bring up my horse, I will leave this inhospitable roof."

He drew himself up proudly and turned to Jim, who advanced with a placating smile.

"No, no, Uncle Randolph," he protested, "we can't let you go like this. Come into the kitchen and Damaris will get your breakfast. You're too weak to go out in the heat."

"Well, I am weak," admitted the old man as he tottered toward the door. "Something struck me . . . on the head."

"You fell off your horse," explained Chatfield. "We had to carry you in."

"And where is that assassin that was shooting at

me?" demanded Morgan, suddenly remembering his approach to the ranch. "He's a Tolliver! I know it! They've followed me even here! But I'll kill him . . . I'll fight to the death!"

"No, no, Uncle," soothed Jim, "that was only Riley Sloper. He was out of his head with the heat."

"No, he wasn't," denied Morgan. "I knew his father well. The worst killer in the whole damned crew."

"Well, he's gone," lied Chatfield, "so come in and wash up. Don't you remember my father, Oliver Chatfield?"

"What? Oliver's son?" exclaimed the old man incredulously. "Why, of course I know you now. Why, Jim, I'm glad to see you. You must tell me about my old friend."

He shuffled along after Jim, talking garrulously about Oliver Chatfield and quite diverted from his purpose.

As the door closed behind them, Riley Sloper appeared and beckoned Lightfoot outside.

"Ain't that Frying-Pan George?" he asked mysteriously. "Well, this puts me in a hell of a fix. I done called off our feud . . . and I meant it, too. But if that old man finds out I'm one of Bodie's men, he'll go to shooting instanter. And I'd shore hate to kill a Chatfield now."

"Wait a minute," said Johnny. "Are you strong enough to ride?"

When Sloper said he was, Lightfoot slipped inside for a word with Jim Chatfield.

"He'll stake you to a horse," Lightfoot said, coming back. "But you'll have to leave your guns behind."

"I'll leave anything," promised Sloper, "not to

break my word to Jim after all this bad blood and killing. I'm a changed man now, and I'm going back to Kaintuck to tell 'em about little Jim."

"Come on, then," suggested Lightfoot, "and I'll give you an Indian pony."

But as he was leading out the horse, Morgan's quick ear heard its steps and he thrust his shaggy head out the door.

"You'd better be drifting," Lightfoot advised Sloper quietly, holding the pony for him to mount.

Sloper swung up into the saddle.

"Who is that man?" demanded old Morgan sharply, squinting after him with purblind eyes. "Why, isn't that Riley Sloper?"

"Yes, it is," answered Lightfoot, coming up. "He came here to get his horse. Good bye, Riley!" He waved his hand.

"Hell and destruction!" raved Morgan, making a run to find his guns. "That's a spy! He's a Bodie man! Jim Chatfield, come out here and shoot that scoundrelly whelp!"

But Chatfield was nowhere to be found, and Sloper went whipping up the road.

"Lord Almighty!" wailed the old man as he rushed out to the gate. "He got away, in spite of me! Why, that hound of a Tolliver has thrown in with Val Bodie in order to get his revenge. And now, by the gods, he'll ride back to Mormon Lake and tell Bodie the way is clear!"

"What way?" inquired Chatfield, coming out with his gun.

The old man was consumed with rage. "Why, the way to my mine!" he shrilled. "The way to the lost Breyfogle, the richest mine in the world! Ride after him, Jim, and kill him!"

"I can't do it," responded Chatfield. "He's a Tolliver, Uncle, and I've promised never to fight them again."

"Then I'll ride him down myself!" raved Morgan, running back to saddle his horse. But as he swung up to mount, the exertion overcame him, and he fell back senselessly on the ground.

"Poor old man," said Jim. "He's crazy."

But, for the first time, Johnny Lightfoot doubted it.

Chapter Twenty-eight

To Chatfield, to Damaris—even to Diana, his daughter—Randolph Morgan seemed out of his head. But Lightfoot had seen the gold that he had dug and he knew that his fears were sound. Riley Sloper had fled up the trail toward Mormon Lake, and, if he even mentioned the presence of Frying-Pan George, Val Bodie would guess the rest. For if Morgan had left his cañon, the gateway lay open—and the madman who guarded the heights was gone.

Lightfoot paced about uneasily as the women and Chatfield sought to pacify the stubborn old man.

"I'll go back to your mine," he offered, "and hold it until you come."

"No! I'll go back myself!" stormed Morgan. "I'm perfectly well! Let me go!"

"No, Uncle!" protested Damaris. "You've had a hard fall and injured your head on a rock. And, besides, you couldn't stand the heat. Now just lie down and be still."

Morgan lay back with a groan, but as evening came on, he sent word for Lightfoot to come.

"Young man," he began, "I am informed by my nephew that you are a person of some integrity. Perhaps my daughter was to blame, in part, for your conduct. Can I trust you to hold my mine?"

"You can if you treat me right and quit talking

about your daughter," answered Lightfoot, glancing at Damaris. "But if you folks say much more about my conduct, and Diana, I'm going to step up on my horse and go."

"Oh, now, Mister Lightfoot," spoke up Damaris reproachfully, "just because I happened to warn her not to go too far . . . is that any reason to complain? You know that poor Diana has spent her life in that narrow cañon without any mother to advise her, and I consider it my duty to take a mother's place and tell her about the ways of the world."

"Well, dog-gone it, can't you trust me?" he flared back angrily. "We were getting along fine . . . we were friends. But now, every time I look at her, she blushes and runs away. What have I ever done more than kiss her once or twice that time when her old man tried to kill me? I reckon I've got a right to talk to her, haven't I? Well, I haven't spoken a word to her today."

"Diana is very tired," stated Damaris, "and Jim and I thought she should rest. But we didn't ask you in to discuss our cousin's affairs. Uncle Randolph wants to talk about his mine."

She waved her hand toward the old man, who was listening impatiently, and dragged Jim out of the room.

"Never mind her!" spoke up Morgan. "She's only a woman. Now what do you know of my mine?"

"It looked good to me, when I was up there," replied Lightfoot. "And Diana showed me some of the ore."

"She did!" exclaimed Morgan. "But never mind . . . never mind. Do you think that Val Bodie will steal it?"

"If he hears that cañon is open, he'll be up it like

a shot. That's why I say I'd better go and take care of it."

"Yes, but what assurance have I that you won't keep it for yourself, and put me to the trouble of evicting you? I remember you now, suh, and you came into this country on purpose to look for the Breyfogle."

"Sure did," admitted Johnny. "But I didn't look any farther after I'd seen a piece of your ore. I could have stolen the mine then, if I wanted to."

"You could not!" Morgan glared. "And for the very good reason that I was there and in full possession. Moreover, my claim is staked and I've kept up the assessment work. And if you'd tried to take possession, I'd have killed you."

"You came damned near doing it as it was," retorted Lightfoot. "Now what do you want me to do?"

"I want you," said Morgan, "to convince these folks that I'm not out of my head. And then we'll go back to the cañon."

"You lie down and go to sleep and quit arguing the matter, and they won't need any convincing," replied Johnny. "And the way things are breaking, I'll be glad to go along with you. In fact, I was about to go anyhow."

"They're just crazed by the heat, and the excitement," confided Morgan. "Don't you mind what Jim's wife has to say. She's a good-hearted woman, but bossy, like all of 'em. Let 'em talk . . . it don't hurt . . . and then go ahead and have your own way."

"I'll remember that," promised Lightfoot grimly. "What time do you want to start?"

"At midnight." Morgan winked. "While they're

all asleep. And, young man, I'll tell you what I'll
do. You stand by me faithfully in this trouble with
Val Bodie, and I'll give you that horse you stole.
Yes, Paynim . . . sired by Selim, out of Neysa . . .
two of the finest English thoroughbreds in the Stud
Book."

"I'll go you on that," responded Johnny, shaking
hands. But the old man would not let him go.

"One thing more," he said. "Leave that Injun at
home. He's a Schooshonnie, and the whole breed is
treacherous. In horses and men alike I've never
known it to fail . . . a low strain is always base. It's
blood that counts . . . and by the way, Lightfoot,
that's a good old Southern name you have. Would
you mind telling me a little about your people?
The pardonable anxiety of a father, you understand. I'm still concerned for the welfare of my
daughter."

"Well, my old man was a lawyer in Austin, Texas
and he tried to make a lawyer out of me. That's
all . . . except that I ran away."

"I see," observed Morgan. "And you're not a fugitive from justice?"

"I never look behind me," answered Lightfoot
bluntly.

The old man clapped him on the shoulder.
"Enough said!" He nodded. "You're the very man
I want. We'll start for the cañon at midnight."

Johnny slipped out the door and made his way
to the corral, where the horses were kept for the
night, but, although Paynim came forward and
whickered eagerly, he put his rope on High Behind. He was a rough horse and an awkward one,
with his high rump and straddling gait, but he was
Johnny's own, and the young man took him. He

had decided to leave anyway, and another bout with Bodie would only serve to work off his spleen. But as he lay in the hay, awaiting the hour to start, he gazed at Paynim and sighed.

A thoroughbred, sired by Selim, with a pedigree that went back to Darley's Arab and likely the God-olphin Barb. And he had taken him for a mustang—a broomtail. Once more he remembered the ecstasy that had thrilled him as he watched Paynim come galloping across the lake. How his mane had floated out as, like a creature of the night, he had led his *manada* to the water hole. And with what a wild whistle he had greeted the mustangers when they whipped in to make their throws. But the horse never lived that could outrun Paynim. Yet Johnny had tied to him, at last.

What a fever he had lived in through these long months that had followed—of chasing and racing and skirmishes with Bodie, and flights for his life from Morgan. It was a rough country and a hard one, with no law but the knife and gun, and he had won only to lose at the end. What Morgan's rifle and barricade had failed to accomplish, Diana's relatives had achieved in a day. She was afraid of him now, abashed in his presence—ashamed, perhaps, for what she had done. And so, by their talk, they had destroyed her childish innocence as ruthlessly as trampling on a flower.

He remembered Diana, the simple child of Na-ture who had kissed him as if he had been her own brother, a creature of joyous moods and wild, law-less impulses, but kind and generous to a fault. What a pity that they had plucked her so ruthlessly away from him with stern warnings against all mankind. Now he must go away and let her blush unseen until the memory of her innocence had lost its pang. But she would never be the old Diana again with her childish longings to be loved.

Lightfoot sighed and stretched out for a little sleep before the long, hard ride to Devil's Cañon. When the Big Dipper rose high in the north, he roused up and saddled the horses. Morgan came out bringing his rifle and six-shooters, which he had retrieved from Chatfield's room, and, leading out their mounts, they rode off up the trail that led to Enúpi Kai. He who twice before had fled from Morgan's vengeance now rode beside him, armed.

If Val Bodie arrived first, there would be a battle or a killing—a plain murder at the mouth of the cañon. For Bodie could not prove a clear title to the mine while Randolph Morgan lived, and the shortest way for him was the one he would take—a cold-blooded assassination at the gateway. They rode fast, for the valley floor had cooled at last as the cold air from the upper country sucked down into the sink, forcing out the superheated vapors. The terrible heat had passed, and, as Morgan saw his mountain before him, his obsession returned.

"They'll be there! I know it!" he cried again and again as they loped along through the night. "They've set out to rob me, the whole devilish crew! But a Morgan never surrenders. If they've taken my mine, I'll take it back or know the reason. And if I get there first, I'll blast down the north wall and block the gateway again!"

"All right," responded Lightfoot. "Only let me get out first. All I ask is an open road . . . and Paynim."

"He's a noble horse," praised Morgan. "One horse in a million. A horse with the courage of a man. But I sized you up rightly the first time I saw you . . . you're a man that loves a horse."

"That's right," agreed Lightfoot. "And I'll take good care of him. I wouldn't bring him on this trip because the bullets will be flying. I've felt it in my bones, from the first."

"Then whip up that deformed creature and show some speed!" exclaimed Morgan. "There's a fortune at stake, so ride! What a damned imposition, to keep me lying there in bed while that spy was riding back to Bodie! She's a Tolliver, that woman . . . I distrusted her from the start! And she leads Jim Chatfield around by the nose as if he had lost his wits. Why, just a word from him and she'd have gone back where she belonged and left men's affairs to her betters. Whip up, I say, and ride!"

He put Turco to a gallop and Johnny followed closely, while the old man cursed and raved. Morgan's giant strength had returned, and his fiery hatred of opposition, and Lightfoot kept discreetly in the rear. He was taking a chance, riding out with this madman who twice before had attempted his life, but chances were what men lived by in that Valley of Death, and they rode until the dawn touched the eastern horizon.

The knife-like edge of Devil's Mountain stood out clearly against the sky as they came within sight of the lake, but Lost Valley was empty and deserted. Across the alkali flats to the west the wild burros came plodding in, and a raven flew down from the cliffs. It passed low, with rushing wings and beady black eyes, looking them over like the ghoul it was, but Morgan did not follow its flight. His desert-trained eyes were searching the wide valley, and at last he pointed to the north.

"There go my horses," he exclaimed, "pulling out for Mesquite Spring! The feed's short up the cañon, and they've been shut up all summer. Let's ride up and turn them back!"

"What's the matter with going up the cañon first?" suggested Johnny. "You can round up your horses any time."

"That's not as easy as you think," replied Morgan shortly. "This is the second time they've turned wild. They love the open country and may be gone for months. They're racers, and they're bound to have their run."

He took after them furiously, thinking nothing of Turco's weariness as he spurred him across the water-soaked flats, but at sight of their master the golden horses hoisted their tails and sped away in full flight. Lightfoot followed reluctantly, ready to aid in the drive if Morgan happened to turn them back, but they fled before his charge, kicking their heels up mischievously, and Turco lagged farther behind. He raised his head and neighed as he saw his beloved companions setting forth on their gay adventure, but the hard gallop had sapped his strength and he only grunted at the bite of the spurs.

"They've quit me!" yelled Morgan, whirling his horse to look back. And then, while he stared, his jaw fell. "What's that," he cried, "coming down out of Daylight Cañon? It's Val Bodie . . . they're after my mine!"

He pointed a tremulous finger and Lightfoot saw them riding—a long procession of horsemen, rushing down out of the eastern cañon and up across the washes to the north. They rode hard, dwarfed by distance till they looked like a column of ants on their way to some new-found honey pot. And up in front, on his bay racer, Val Bodie led the gang as they swarmed into the mouth of Devil's Cañon.

Chapter Twenty-nine

Through his own bull-headedness, Morgan had thrown away his chance to become the defender of his mine. He had ridden off to turn back his runaway horses, and now he had lost them both.

In a paroxysm of rage he sat watching the claim jumpers as they poured into the mouth of the cañon, while his beard wagged in time to the gusty oaths that flowed from his mouth in a torrent.

He cursed the horses, and Turco, and Jim Chatfield's woman who had kept him in bed like a child, and then, whipping Turco until he lashed him into a fury, he headed for Devil's Cañon at a gallop.

Lightfoot followed after him, debating in his mind whether to turn back or see the thing through. If they had gained the cañon first, Morgan's berserk rage would have served a useful purpose. With his rifle and six-shooters, and his name for a fighter, he could easily have turned back the night riders. But now he was charging into the mouth of a cañon that was defended by sixteen gunmen, the most desperate killers on the desert. Lightfoot lagged behind dubiously, scanning the cliffs for an ambush, but Morgan plunged in boldly.

In a long, expectant silence, Lightfoot awaited the volley that would spell the old man's end. When it came, he would know that Bodie had accomplished his purpose, but the only sound was the *clank* of shod hoofs. They had passed in, all of them, unaware of the devil man's presence, intent only on the rich loot ahead.

After a long minute of waiting, Lightfoot leaned forward and jumped High Behind into a lope. The way was clear, and Morgan still had a chance to gain back his treasure and his mine. But he could not win alone—the odds were too great—and Lightfoot had promised his help. For the horse that he loved he had given his word to ride with Randolph Morgan to his mine, and now, with all danger of ambush past, he spurred in to do his part.

Up the narrow, crooked passageway with its towering walls on both sides he followed on the jump. But as he approached the cave, there was an outbreak of shooting and two riderless horses dashed past. Lightfoot gave them the trail, his pistol balanced to shoot, if the battle came his way. Then, as the loud *bang* of a horse pistol set his heart to pounding wildly, he whooped and charged out into the open.

Before the mouth of the cave a group of men stood peering in. The ground was strewn with the plunder they had taken. But at sight of Lightfoot, riding in from down the cañon, they broke and ran for the rocks. Then, from inside the cavern, the shooting broke out afresh, and two men came rushing forth. Lightfoot whipped out his six-shooter and met their charge with a smashing bullet that threw up the dust at their feet, and they dropped their guns and ran.

There was a panic in the cañon, with men running to and fro and frightened horses splashing madly through the creek. And from within the dark cave a succession of muffled shots told Johnny that Morgan still lived. He came out on the instant, a smoking horse pistol in each hand, stooping low to escape the expected shots. But at sight of Johnny, still mounted on High Behind, he straightened up and looked swiftly around.

"Oh! You here, eh?" he grunted, thrusting one pistol into its holster while he shoved cartridges into the other. "The rascals were looting my home. Look at these sacks of ore that they had lugged out into the open and threw away to hunt for more gold. But there are two of them inside that will never steal again. Ketch my horse . . . we'll go up to the mine."

Lightfoot rounded up Turco, who had gone down to drink. His brain was still in a whirl. Was it possible that one old man could whip single-handed this whole gang of thieves and claim jumpers? He had scattered a good half of them at his first reckless charge. But where were Bodie and the Boots brothers?

"Mister Morgan," he warned, "you want to look out now, because Bodie is up at the mine."

"That's why I'm going up there," returned Morgan tartly. "If you're afraid of getting killed . . . stay behind!"

"I'm not afraid," answered Johnny. "But Bodie will hear this shooting. And the Boots boys are up there, too."

"What do I care for them, the half-Injun whelps?" cursed Morgan as he swung up on his horse. "Val Bodie will fight . . . he's a white man!"

"Yes, and Hank Boots will fight!" put in Lightfoot. "Do you figure you can handle them both?"

"Well, you come along and tend to Hank," proposed Morgan, "and I'll tell you what I'll do. The whole gang will be up there, and they'll fight to hold that mine. But we can whip 'em if I can just down Bodie. Now you watch Hank. I'll do the rest. If we win, you get half the mine."

Lightfoot stared at him curiously, for the crackbrained old prospector had suddenly been transformed into a strategist. The light of battle was in his eyes; he moved about quickly—and for the first time since Johnny had known him he seemed sane. Yet the odds were all against them, for every one of the Boots boys could shoot. They had been educated by their father for just such emergencies.

"What's to keep them from potting us with their rifles," he demanded, "before we get close enough to shoot? I'm in favor of going up on foot."

"Young man," began Morgan, "I'm experienced in these matters. I'd killed men before you were born. Now you ain't hired to think. You do what I say and I'll give you half my mine."

"To hell with the mine!" retorted Lightfoot. "What good will it do me if I'm dead? I claim those Indians will fight. . . ."

"Let 'em fight!" stormed Morgan. "What the devil will we be doing? But I know Bodie, and he'll want to make a talk. And once I get him talking, I'll walk closer. You stay on your horse, like you wasn't called in on it . . . you're a witness while I stake my mine. But when you hear me say . . . 'law!' . . . you tend to Hank Boots. Because right then I'm going to kill Bodie." He nodded his head and turned imperiously away.

After a moment's hesitation Lightfoot followed, for he could not go back on his word. Yet as he rode up the cañon, he felt like a leaf drawn in behind the rush of horses' hoofs. He had not counted on a battle so desperate when he had offered to go to the mine, nor would it have been necessary if Morgan's runaway horses had not diverted him from his purpose. Once safely inside the gateway, they could have withstood the charge of 100 outlaws like Bodie, but the cards had fallen against them, and now, willy-nilly, he was being drawn into a fight to the death. For Bodie and Hank Boots would shoot, and so would Boots's half-breed sons. But Morgan rode out against them blithely.

Up the cañon the cloudburst had swept away the trail that led to the hidden mine, but as they rounded the point and turned up the side cañon, they saw Bodie at the tunnel mouth. He stood waiting, his rifle ready to shoot, but Morgan came on confidently, ignoring Hank Boots and his sons. Always before, as Frying-Pan George, he had been loud-mouthed and violent, full of windy threats against the first man that jumped his mine. But in the presence of the actual jumpers he was calm. Bodie watched him narrowly—and Lightfoot, riding behind—until they came to the edge of the claim. Then he stepped out and held up his hand.

"Stop right there!" he ordered. "You're trespassing on my ground."

But Morgan rode in on him arrogantly.

"You're a liar!" he answered. "I've owned this mine for years."

"Hey! Stop!" yelled Bodie, whipping his gun up to his shoulder. "Or I'll bore you through and through. There wasn't a stake or monument on the whole damned claim. And what's more, it's never been recorded."

"That's all right," argued Morgan. "I've got a witness here to prove that the claim was legally staked. That cloudburst came down and washed my monuments away. I order you off of my ground!"

He stepped down off his horse and advanced across the open while Lightfoot, like a man in a dream, edged his horse out of the line of fire. It was impossible to believe that Morgan planned an open attack, that at any moment he might draw and fire. But Lightfoot had seen him at the battle of the cave and he set himself for the fray. For before Morgan fired, if he lived up to his promise, he was to speak the one word—*law*.

Bodie stood there, huge and glowering, his rifle ready to shoot, his henchmen lined up at his side—Hank Boots, tall and lanky, Big John, with Pete behind him, and Injun Boots, black and evil-eyed. They were startled by the actions of Frying-Pan George, and Hank Boots had cocked his rifle. But Morgan came on, oblivious of them all, his fierce eyes fixed on Bodie.

"Val Bodie," he began, "you've been trying for ten years to rob me of my mine. But I tell you, right now, I won't stand it!"

Boots spoke in Bodie's ear, and his big rifle came up.

"Halt!" he commanded. "You murdering old renegade! You ain't got no mine! I done located it, I tell you!"

He stopped, and his gunmen spread out. A sudden hush came over them all, and Johnny knew the moment had come. They were set to shoot the old man down. Randolph Morgan sensed it, too, but he did not give an inch.

"You Mormon whelp!" he cursed. "You think you can steal it, do you? I came into this country before there was any law. . . ." He leaped aside as he spoke the word and Lightfoot saw Hank Boots lay his cheek against the stock of his rifle. Then Morgan's pistol went off and Johnny drew and shot before Boots could pull the trigger. Their two shots rang out like two cracks of a whip and Bodie and Hank Boots staggered back. Bodie swayed and fell sidewise, Boots toppled over backward, and his three half-breed sons stood alone. Lightfoot caught a glimpse of their evil, staring eyes as they ducked and went for their guns. Then High Behind rose up in a resistless, whirling buck and Johnny felt himself hurled to the ground.

He hit hard, dropping his pistol, and, as he leaped up to a crouch, he saw the Boots brothers running. Morgan had charged them intolerantly, contemptuous of their rifles. Injun Boots fell, then turned over and whipped out his gun. Big John and the youthful Pete were fleeing together down the hill, when, with the vengeful swiftness of a rattlesnake, Injun Boots aimed and fired, shooting Morgan in the back as he passed.

It was all over in an instant, and, as Morgan fell, Lightfoot groped about for his gun. A bullet ripped down his shoulder blade, burning its way like a streak of fire, and he rose up to find Injun Boots fanning. It was a trick he had learned from his renegade father, holding the trigger back firmly while he aimed from the hip and worked the hammer with the flat of his left hand.

A second bullet struck Johnny, whirling him around and destroying his aim, but he came up shooting and, as they closed in to fight it out, Injun Boots stumbled forward and fell. But Johnny had seen the trick by which he had shot Morgan, and he turned and emptied his gun. Then a giddiness seized him and he seemed to be falling through infinite space, until suddenly his light went out.

Chapter Thirty

All the devils from hell seemed to be working on Johnny Lightfoot, searing his back with a rod of fire, smashing in his ribs with mighty blows, choking off his breath until he struggled and woke up.

He was lying alone before the mouth of Morgan's mine—the others who sprawled there were dead men. He gazed about dumbly, wiping the dirt from his bloodshot eyes, and from the distance a lost horse neighed. It was Turco, still waiting for his master.

A battle had been fought, but the vanquished had fled and the sole survivor lay weltering in blood. There was a trench down his back, and at every labored breath a broken rib stabbed into his side, yet as he reared up, he cursed the folly of it all. What to him was the Lost Breyfogle, when for one drink of water he would give his hope of salvation? It had not been his quarrel—he had been drawn into it against his will—and now Morgan and Bodie were both dead. Two more names added to the long list of men who had perished in the search for gold. And Hank Boots and his son made four more.

Like the dancing figures of a fever dream, Lightfoot envisioned once more the swift action of that desperate fight—Bodie and Hank Boots shot down together, outguessed at their own game, and then Morgan's overweening charge. But the cunning of

Injun Boots had given him a quick revenge for the death of his father and Bodie. He alone had kept his head—and, as Morgan fell, the half-breed had turned his spitting pistol on Lightfoot. There was nothing for Lightfoot then but to shoot. Now that it was over he felt sick.

The horse whinnied again and Lightfoot called to him hopefully. Then, as Turco refused to come, he crawled down toward him slowly, one hand pressed tightly against his side. It was the broken rib that hurt him, but each time he stopped, Turco whinnied a frenzied appeal. It was his nature to be loyal and, now that his master was dead, he had transferred his allegiance to Lightfoot.

Turco was standing in the wash where at the first outbreak of shooting he had been stampeded by the frightened High Behind. But old High Behind had never stopped, for once before at Night Water he had felt the raking impact of buckshot, and Turco waited alone. It cost Lightfoot many a groaning to crawl on Turco's back and ride back to the deserted cave, and there, as Turco turned his head down the cañon, Johnny read what was in the animal's heart.

Far below in the wide valley his brethren were running free, seeking out a new range to the north. Loosening the saddle, Lightfoot stripped off the bridle and slapped him over the rump with the reins.

"Go ketch 'em, old boy," he said. "I wish I was going with you." And Turco set off, although doubtfully. He paused and looked back—then, in a quick, joyous gallop, he dashed away down the trail.

Lightfoot stood alone in the deserted cañon, one

hand against his side, a single gun on his hip, and in the distance he heard men's voices, shouting. Somewhere among the rocks or on the lofty cliffs the scattered night riders were calling. He dodged into the cave, where amid the ruins of Morgan's home two dead men lay against the wall, and came out with a sack of jerked meat. Then, filling a canteen, he crept back into his old hiding place and concealed his tracks behind him.

In the battle at the mine he had come off victor, since he alone had survived, but if, sick and wounded, he fell into the enemies' hands, there would be a different story to tell. In the cool darkness of the cave, he stretched out behind the packing boxes that had given him cover before, and after a drink from the canteen he fell into a fevered sleep, interrupted by the sound of passing footsteps. Harsh voices came to his ears and the *clack* of horses' hoofs. Then, as night came on and the bats fluttered forth, the ancient stillness returned.

He was awakened by the padding of some animal in his cave, and, as he opened his eyes, he saw a fox running out, while another stood gazing at him curiously. It was Christopher and Columbus, Diana's pet foxes—they had scented his jerked meat and come in. Or had they some remembrance of a former friendship, expressed by the faint wagging of their tails? Johnny tried to sit up, to reach behind him for the meat sack, but his back seemed clamped in a bar of iron. The bullet furrow had become stiff, and the pain in his side made him wince and gasp for breath.

He lay back, muttering, cursing the luck that had led him to this spot. Once before, filled with buckshot, he had awakened in this same cave and seen the bats flapping home with the dawn. But now there was no Diana to tend his stiffening wounds—he was alone, and his enemies were about. The foxes raced to the door as two horses came hammering up, and from his couch Lightfoot could see their eager heads outstretched as they sniffed the wind from below. Then Christopher, the boldest, stepped out into the light.

"H'lo!" hailed a rough voice, and the foxes scurried away as swiftly as two flashes of light. One moment they had been there and the next they were gone. Lightfoot reached for his pistol and waited. Then silence, the sound of distant footsteps coming closer, and a head peered into the cave. It was Diana, and she was crying.

"Oh, Johnny!" she called. "Johnny, dear!" And Lightfoot felt suddenly confounded. Diana had followed after him, but how could he meet her—how tell her of her father's death? But at the tenderness in her voice, the quavering word of endearment, his heart leaped within him for joy.

"Johnny!" she cried hopefully, and, when he answered from his hiding place, she stooped and ran into the cave. "Oh, are you here, Johnny?" she sobbed as she reached gropingly toward the form on the old, familiar couch. "Is it really you, Johnny? Aren't you killed?"

"Nope . . . I'm all right," responded Lightfoot. "Just got raked by a couple of bullets."

She found him in the darkness, and, as her hands touched his cheeks, she leaned down suddenly and kissed him.

"I'm so glad." She sighed. "So glad you're still alive. And I'll never be mean to you again. But . . . but where is Father, Johnny?"

She asked the question bravely, but Johnny could see she knew the answer, and he told his story bluntly.

"We had a battle at the mine and he was killed," he said. "But he got Val Bodie first."

"Oh, and then you, Johnny?" she hurried on. "Were you there in the fighting? And did Bodie's men try to kill you?"

"Sure did," admitted Lightfoot. "But that's all over now. Who was that I heard talking outside?"

"It was Captain Jack," she answered. "But when he looked into the cave and saw those two dead men lying there, he was scared and ran away. We thought they were you and Father."

"Couple of Bodie's men," he explained. "They were robbing the house. But you'd better not go back there."

"No, no," she promised. "I'll stay right here with you till Cousin Jim gets in. Jack and I rode ahead . . . we had Paynim and Moonbeam. But why did you do it, Johnny?"

"I don't know," responded Lightfoot. "Seemed like luck was against me . . . and I couldn't let him come up alone. We'd've been all right, at that, but he saw your horses pulling out. And when we got back . . . here was Bodie!"

"Poor Father." She sighed again. "But I knew he'd get killed . . . I told him so, hundreds of times. They were terrible men to deal with."

"The worst in the country," he agreed. "There's your little fox at the door."

She turned, and, as Christopher ran forward to greet her, she gathered him into her arms like a child.

"Oh, I'm so glad!" she sobbed. "And here's Columbus, too! Before I saw them I thought you were dead. Then they ran out of the cave and I remembered how they loved you, Johnny."

She pushed them both away and leaned down close to Lightfoot, and then she laid her cheek against his.

"And I love you, too," she whispered. "I don't care what they say."

Chapter Thirty-one

Jim Chatfield came riding in, to protect his cousin's property and attend to the wounded and dead—and then Damaris, to be a mother to Diana.

An adobe house rose up, to take the place of the old cave, and Diana appeared demurely in long skirts.

Captain Jack brought his woman and camped among the willows, but Johnny Lightfoot lived on in his cave. There, as the bats winged in and out and the foxes came to greet him and beg for more meat from his store, he lay dreaming till his back got well. But it was Jim who tended him now.

Diana was changed, and every day Lightfoot could hear Damaris, talking to her. She was a good woman—a good mother to such as little Jim—but Johnny thought she talked too much. She had reminded him more than once that Diana was related to some of the best families in Kentucky, and Jim had shown him one diamond from the casket that Diana had snatched when she had fled. It was large and a pure bluish white. Yet Lightfoot knew he was welcome, for Diana had a smile in her eyes. And, of course, he had saved the mine.

The Lost Breyfogle lay just as it was, after the cloudburst and the battle had swept over it. To Diana its black depths were haunted by memories of her father and his wasted life—and four men had died at its mouth. In other matters she deferred meekly to the judgment of her cousins, but she ordered the tunnel closed. And, of course, after all, it was her mine—although Jim thought it ought to be worked.

There was talk already of a trip back to Kentucky to celebrate the end of the feud, and Diana would need the money. For while she was there, of course, she would have social opportunities that had been denied her in Devil's Cañon. Damaris gave herself up to an orgy of sewing and fitting, for Diana must look her best, and sometimes, in the evening, Lightfoot glimpsed the filmy gowns that now replaced her buckskin suit. But Damaris was always present and Johnny did not linger, although they always invited him to stay.

He was rebuilding the pasture fence, which the flood had swept away, and putting in a new gate and stile. It was just like the stile that had been there before, when Diana had given him the kiss. He often sat there in the evening while Paynim and Moonbeam came down to stand at the bars, and, when they looked down the cañon and sniffed the wind, he knew where their thoughts had strayed. Somewhere outside the portals that shut them in, their runaway companions were playing. They were racing across the *playas* of distant dry lakes or mingling with the mustangs on the plains, but someday they would all come back.

The cool of autumn came, and, as the heat fever left his brain, Lightfoot felt a strange content. Why should he seek to placate the designing Damaris, or show resentment when she kept Diana close? Diana had kissed him and told him that she loved him, no matter what they said. She had placed her cheek against his, alone there in the cave, and told him he was very dear. And the look in her eyes was the same, only now it was hidden and veiled.

But the open ranges were calling and he got out his plaited throw rope. Diana did not need him in the cañon now, for Chatfield would protect her mine, but somewhere, running wild, were the nine golden horses, which she watched for day by day. Every evening, with her foxes, when the sun was swinging low, Diana went up the trail to her old look-out on the cliff. But Johnny did not dare to follow. The motherly eyes of Damaris were never long off the foot of that trail, and she had her opinion of horse hunters.

Johnny overhauled his saddle and put in new latigos and limbered up his reata with tallow. Then he whipped it on the ground to straighten out the kinks and made delicate casts at High Behind. And he, although he had twice proved a recreant before gunfire, stood his ground and snorted to go. He was a good horse and a tough one on the trail after mustangs, and he knew the signs of a hunt. But Lightfoot did not go.

The moon was at its full, the favorite hunting time for mustangers, and a cool wind sucked up from below. That evening, as Johnny came back from the pasture, he saw Diana, skipping lightly down her trail. Her cumbersome skirts were held high—she came down gaily, almost dancing—and, when she spied him, she waved her hand. Johnny glanced at the house, where Damaris was getting supper, and hurried to meet her, for he guessed the news.

"They've come back!" she said. "I saw them . . . down at Night Water. I'll meet you at midnight, Johnny."

She slipped into the house, and Lightfoot walked on air as he sought the shelter of his cave. It was the old Diana, the Diana who had kissed him and dared him to ride through the night—and her eyes had been alight like stars. All the chatter of Damaris had not altered her a whit, when it came to a ride on the lake. She had let her aunt talk, and now, like with her father, she would go ahead and, have her own way.

The foxes followed after him as Lightfoot went down the trail with his saddle and rigging on his arm, and, as he sat by the gate, the horses came down and nudged him with pleadings to go. Then the moon soared up and shone down into the cañon, and Lightfoot's heart stood still. On such a night as this how could she deny him? And yet he could not ask for a kiss. They were hers to give, if she would.

She came at last, gliding silently in her moccasins and with her golden hair thrown to the wind. It seemed in a way the symbol of her freedom, like her buckskin leggings and short skirt.

"Oh, Johnny." She sighed ecstatically. "I just couldn't stay at home. There were Turco and Selim and all of them. Just think of all the mustangers that have been trying to catch them . . . and every one came back."

"I'll ketch 'em," promised Lightfoot, "if you'll let me ride on Paynim."

"Why, of course! He's yours!" she answered joyously. "Didn't I give him to you long ago?"

"Well, yes," he admitted. "But Jim and your cousin Damaris. . . ."

"Oh, come on!" she cried.

She scrambled lightly over the bars and put her

bridle on Moonbeam, while Lightfoot led out Paynim, and then, closing the gate against the sulky High Behind, they rode away down the dark, moonstruck cañon. Across patches of moonlight they spied Christopher and Columbus, gliding ahead like silver-gray shadows, and Diana laughed for joy.

"Isn't it wonderful?" she said. "Oh, I never was so happy! I was afraid they'd never come back!"

"I was going out after them," answered Lightfoot soberly. "Kind of shut in like . . . up in that cañon."

"We're out of it!" she exulted, jumping Moonbeam into a gallop and tearing away down the wash, and, as Johnny leaned forward, Paynim dashed up beside her and led on till they came to the dry lake.

It lay like a silvery sea, bathed in tropical moonlight, with the mystery of the desert brooding over it—smooth and hard as a racetrack. And from far across the flats there came the braying of wild burros as they carried on their endless battles. Diana reined in, panting, knee to knee with Lightfoot as he peered out into the night, but he did not take her hand. Paynim had thrown up his head, eagerly sniffing the breeze. From the distance there came a high, shrill whistle.

"Plumb wild," he said. "They'll run like a blacktail . . . been chased all over Nevada. You'll never ride up to them, Diana."

"Yes, I will!" she insisted. "I raised them from colts, Johnny. Just let me do it my way."

"Well, sure," he agreed. "But they've turned wild, I tell you. You should have seen 'em when they ran away from your father."

"Oh, but, Johnny," she protested, "you know they were frightened then. Take your hand off of Paynim's nose."

Lightfoot obeyed reluctantly, and across the empty lakebed Paynim sent his high, challenging neigh. Another stallion made answer and in the stillness of the night they heard his loud, explosive snort.

"That's Turco," spoke up Diana. "He's angry."

"Yes, and Paynim is angry, too," answered Lightfoot. "If they once start to fighting, I'm ditched, so you'd better ride in alone."

"No! Now, Johnny," she pleaded, "I want you to be with me when we catch them and drive them home. I had it all planned out."

"Well, you'll have to plan again, then," returned Lightfoot. "Because a wild horse doesn't like a man. We've got the wind on 'em now, but the minute they smell me, they'll leave here like bats out of hell."

"All right, then," she came back, "you tell me how to do it. I've known those horses all my life."

"But I haven't," countered Lightfoot, "and they haven't known me. And don't you ever think they'll let me ride up on them, because it's only six months ago that I trapped them by the water hole and put my rope on Paynim. Now you ride out and get acquainted first, and give 'em a good run on the lake. And then I'll show up on the windward side and you lead 'em back up the cañon."

"All right, Johnny," she assented at last, "I suppose you must be right. Only"—she paused and looked wistfully into his eyes—"I wanted you to be with me," she ended.

"Yes, I know." Lightfoot nodded. "We'll ride

home together." And with a light touch he reined his horse away.

Diana rode out slowly, her foxes coursing ahead, mad with joy to be out on the lake, and, as the band of outlaws trotted out on the *playa*, she broke into a joyous gallop. But like one horse they turned and fled and were swallowed up in the night, while she followed, calling their names. From the distance Johnny could see them as they stampeded off, their tails held high like flags and Diana hot on their trail. Then as Paynim fought his head, Lightfoot rode him across the lake and took shelter among the mesquites.

The runaways had turned wild—they were mustangs again—but Paynim and Moonbeam were the top horses of the bunch and would not let them escape. There was a long, anxious wait as Diana rode after them, and then, across the lakebed, came the patter of running hoofs as they circled back from the north. With a rush, half in play, they wheeled and gamboled across the *playa*—a new mare, Cressida, in Moonbeam's place in the lead, Turco herding them proudly from the rear. At sight of his rival, Paynim's wide nostrils flared and he fought against the hackamore on his nose, but Lightfoot choked him down, holding him resolutely back, and Paynim's lost *manada* swept on.

Diana could turn them now, and, as they headed toward the north, Johnny could see her, riding low. Only her golden hair, mingled with Moonbeam's flowing mane, revealed her presence as they came thundering past, and Lightfoot's heart leaped at the memory of that night when first he had seen her. The same moon was shining, the same splendor illumined the *playa*—but now Diana was his.

She would never go back to Kentucky with scheming, match-making Damaris.

He could hear her calling now as she slowed the horses down, edging closer and barring the way to the north, and, as they circled and maneuvered, led on by the jealous Cressida, Moonbeam whinnied to her perfidious children. They had left her for this usurper, the consort of Turco who had ever lived in fear of Paynim's teeth. But not forever could the deposed leader be restrained, and, as Paynim's *manada* passed again, he scorned the biting hackamore and charged.

The time had come to make their drive, if drive them they ever could, and Lightfoot gave his mount his head. But he, too, swung low, clinging to his neck like a bat, and Paynim rushed Turco, bawling. The *manada* was running and they kept on, faster and faster, as that well-remembered challenge rang out. And Turco, although he turned, did not dare to give battle when Paynim rose up to strike. With mouth open and teeth gleaming, his pounding hoofs smashing out, he drove his presumptuous rival in wild flight. Then, circling his little band, Paynim rushed them toward the cañon, and once more Moonbeam dashed into the lead.

Up the wide, gravelly wash and into the black-mouthed portals they went at a breakneck gallop, and, as they entered the narrow cañon, the overhanging walls gave back the echoes of their thunderous flight. Lightfoot rose up, yelling as they swept past the house and found themselves stopped by the gate. He reined Paynim right and left, popping his rope end like a pistol shot as they made futile breaks to escape, while Diana, leaping off, threw down bar after bar until the way into the pasture was clear. Then they poured in, leaping the barrier, and, as Moonbeam passed, Diana swung up on her back.

Lightfoot rode in laughing and put up the bars. Diana circled and came flying back. Then she leaped to the ground and stood beside him, panting, while her arms crept up around his neck.

"Oh, Johnny." She sighed. "I just can't live without you." And she drew his head down for a kiss.

About the Author

Dane Coolidge was born in Natick, Massachusetts. He moved early to northern California with his family and was graduated from Stanford University in 1898. In his summers he worked as a field collector and in 1896 was employed by the British Museum in this capacity in northern Mexico. Coolidge's background as a naturalist is a trademark in his Western fiction along with his personal familiarity with the vast, isolated regions of the American West and its deserts—especially Death Valley. Coolidge married Mary Roberts, a feminist and a professor of sociology at Mills College, in 1906. In the summers, these two ventured among the Indian nations and together they co-authored non-fiction books about the Navajos and the Seris. *Hidden Water* (1910), Coolidge's first Western novel, marked the beginning of a career that saw many of his novels serialized in magazines prior to book publication. There is an extraordinary breadth in these novels from *Wunpost* (1920) set in Death Valley to *Maverick Makers* (1931), a Texas Rangers story. Many of his novels are concerned with prospecting and mining from *Shadow Mountain* (1920) and *Lost Wagons* (1923) based on actual historical episodes in the mining history of Death Valley to a fictional treatment of Colonel Bill Greene's discovery of the fabulous Capote copper mine in Mexico, a central theme in *Wolf's Candle*

(1935) and *Rawhide Johnny* (1936). *The New York Times Book Review* commented on *Hell's Hip Pocket* (1939) that "no other man in the field today writes better Western tales than Dane Coolidge." Coolidge, who died in 1940, wrote with a definite grace and leisurely pace all but lost to the Western story after the Second World War, although Nelson C. Nye, an admirer of Coolidge, tried in his own fiction to capture this same ambiance. The attention to the land and accurate detail make a Dane Coolidge Western story rewarding to readers of any generation.

☐ **YES!**

Sign me up for the Leisure Western Book Club and send my FREE BOOKS! If I choose to stay in the club, I will pay only $14.00* each month, a savings of $9.96!

NAME: _____

ADDRESS: _____

TELEPHONE: _____

EMAIL: _____

☐ I want to pay by credit card.

☐ **VISA** ☐ **MasterCard.** ☐ **DISCOVER**

ACCOUNT #: _____

EXPIRATION DATE: _____

SIGNATURE: _____

Mail this page along with $2.00 shipping and handling to:
Leisure Western Book Club
PO Box 6640
Wayne, PA 19087
Or fax (must include credit card information) to:
610-995-9274
You can also sign up online at **www.dorchesterpub.com**.
*Plus $2.00 for shipping. Offer open to residents of the U.S. and Canada only.
Canadian residents please call 1-800-481-9191 for pricing information.
under 18, a parent or guardian must sign. Terms, prices and conditions subject to change. Subscription subject to acceptance. Dorchester Publishing reserves the right to reject any order or cancel any subscription.